GUARDIANS OF THE FORBIDDEN LIBRARY

THE LAST TEMPLARS - BOOK 2

PRESTON W. CHILD

PROLOGUE

Madison Ainsley was a popular 32-year-old writer of women's romance novels. Most critics agreed she wasn't as good a writer as her father, Culver Ainsley, who authored more than a hundred highly successful detective novels. Their styles and stories could not be more different. According to the Maricopa County Medical Examiner's Office, the same was true of the way they chose to end their lives.

Culver ate a bullet while on vacation in Rome on the 43rd anniversary of the release of his blockbuster first novel. Four months later, Madison checked out using a neater method. She swallowed a brand new bottle of 100 sleeping pills just before going to bed...with the final page of her latest novel still displayed on her computer at her home in Cave Creek, Arizona.

Neither death raised any suspicions officially. After all, suicides among family members—not to mention popular artists—were not uncommon. But one seemingly incidental detail of Madison's case nagged at Maricopa

County Sheriff's Deputy Raymon Byrnes. He was what folks called a "neat freak." His nickname in the department was "Max OCD." And his mind would not let go of the fact that the cap to Madison's bottle of pills was never found. He first noticed its absence in photos of the empty prescription bottle on Madison's nightstand.

No big deal, he thought at first. *It probably ended up on the floor near the bed.*

So he checked the bags of evidence and still didn't find it.

"Let it go!" he admonished himself. "It's no big deal. Whoever collected the evidence probably saw the cap halfway under the bed and never connected it to the empty bottle on the nightstand, or simply missed it altogether. So it never got collected. It's either still under the bed or it got picked up and thrown away when the room was cleaned."

Those possible explanations put the matter to rest for him. But a month later, he had lunch with his FBI Special Agent older brother, Thomas, and unwittingly kicked over a very big rock by asking an innocent question.

"What's shakin', big brother?" Raymon asked.

"Same old shit," Thomas sighed as he stared at his cell phone's screen and typed something.

"Bad day, huh?" Raymon replied. "I'll buy if it cheers you up. If it doesn't, you can buy."

"Actually, I planned to buy," Thomas said, "because I gotta pick your brain about that Ainsley dame who ignored the dosage instructions on the label of her sleeping pills."

"Whadaya wanna know?" Raymon asked, almost relieved to talk about it.

"Didn't she have her book displayed on her computer screen?" Thomas asked.

"Yep, the very end of the story," Raymon said. "But we never told the public."

"Well, another pill-popping writer did the same thing last night in Maine," Thomas said.

"Sleeping pills?" Raymon asked.

"Oxy," Thomas answered. "Strange choice for an 87-year-old guy, ain't it?"

"Who was it?" Raymon asked.

"Andrew William Poitras," Tom answered.

"The gay porn writer?" Raymon asked.

"It's pure art, Ray," Thomas said sarcastically. "Don't you read the tabloids? Do you see anything odd in these photos?"

Raymon looked at the photos of the bottle of Oxy, from close-ups to wide angles.

"No cap!" he blurted out.

"I knew I could count on you," Thomas said with a wry grin. "We still haven't found it. And that made me think of something odd I'd heard at the Bureau about old man Ainsley when he checked out."

"What's that?" Raymon asked.

"They never found the empty shell casing from the pistol he used," Thomas replied softly.

"So what are ya' thinkin?" Ramon asked him.

"I'm thinking we might have a souvenir collector on our hands," Thomas answered.

"Don't you mean a killer who collects souvenirs?" Raymon shot back.

"You are a hopeless stickler for details," Thomas said as his smile turned wicked.

"But what's the connection?" Raymon challenged his brother. "A killer doesn't usually kill for totally useless souvenirs...especially an international killer."

"Well, this is a stretch, but hear me out," Thomas answered. "The only surveillance camera in the hotel Ainsley was staying at in Rome was in the lobby. Only one person entered and left about the time he died. The video of the guy is grainy, but INTERPOL ran a facial recognition scan on him. We believe his name is Lorenzo Mattia Mancini. He has no criminal record, but he has ties to a group that INTERPOL and the Italian police have had on a watch list for a couple of years. They picked him up for questioning and noted he had *Guardian* tattooed on his inside left wrist."

"Guardian?" Raymon repeated. "Guardian of what?"

"Guardians of the Forbidden Library," Thomas answered.

"What the hell is the Forbidden Library?" Raymon asked. "Never heard of it."

"I'm getting to that," Thomas said. "But hear me out. The Bureau asked the field offices for anything they had on the group, and there ain't much nationwide. But the night Madison Ainsley took her last look at her last book, a Cave Creek Patrolman pulled over a guy for speeding three miles from her place. And guess what?"

"He had *Guardian* tattooed on the inside of his left wrist," Raymon answered.

"You play this game very well," Thomas said as his smile turned wry again. "Here are photos of both tattoos."

"They're identical." Raymon stated the obvious.

"Yep," Thomas quipped, "and half a world apart. The Bureau thinks we're onto another radical international organization."

"And they're murdering writers around the world?" Raymon asked incredulously. "I've wanted to murder one or two writers myself over the years. But what's the point of actually doing it? And what does any of this have to do with the missing evidence?"

"I haven't got the slightest idea," Thomas said, "and neither does the Bureau."

"What would you fellas like?" the waitress finally appeared and asked.

"Easy answers," Raymon sighed to the waitress.

"Yeah, I'd like some too," she replied. "But believe me, you can't get any here."

INTRODUCTION

John "Doc" Holiday and his wife, Connie, were surprised by the nostalgia they felt during the few hours they spent in Washington, D.C., with President Preston and the First Lady, Melanie. Yet, even though the luncheon meeting cheered them, they were ready for the flight back to Montana the next morning. In just the few months they'd lived there it had become home. The serene beauty of Flathead Lake, and the warmth of the people living in the small towns around it, provided a welcome change from the crush of crowds and traffic that was D.C.

When the big black Secret Service Suburban turned off of 15th Street, headed for the Willard Inter-Continental Hotel, Doc spotted the Segway rental station on the corner and told Connie he was adding it to his "must do" list for their next trip into town.

"Now that's *my kind of adventure*," Connie said with a smile.

She resisted the urge to voice her concerns about Doc's brand of adventure. She'd made them clear to Doc before they married. But here they were, headed back to their hotel, where Doc would call Q, his best friend and brother-in-arms, to discuss the President's request that they accept another top-secret—and likely dangerous—mission. When the hulking SUV slowed in front of the hotel, Doc asked to be let out at the courtyard, just shy of the front doors, so he could call Q without the worry of someone overhearing the call. Doc made the call on his ultra-secure Blackphone 2 in the open air to get Q's response to the President's request. Though Doc had no details, the President's fear that "world order was at stake" had him on high alert.

As Connie waited in the backseat, she knew the call was a formality. She suspected the President knew it too. They both knew her retired Navy SEAL husband and Q, an "almost-retired" U.S. Marshal, were diehard men of service to the nation. Neither of them could resist a presidential request for their help. So while she waited, she began a mental list of things he'd probably want to pack as soon as they returned to Montana.

"Hey, Q!" Doc began the call casually. "Are you and Marsha, Madeleine, and Noah keeping the home fires burning for us back there?"

"You know it," Q said. "But the next time you ask us to house sit, could you at least have more groceries stocked up? And buy more beer at least?"

"Enjoy my absence while you can, old man," Doc laughed. "We'll be back tomorrow.

In the meantime, I need to know if you're up for another mission you won't be able to talk about."

"Who, what, when, where, and why?" Q asked.

"As always, I don't know yet," Doc sighed. "And what difference does it make? Are you in, or aren't you?"

"You *do* have a way of keeping life interesting," Q laughed. "Let me call you back after I talk with Marsha,"

But at that moment Marsha moved in close, squeezed his arm, and forced a smile.

"Check that," Q quickly said. "I'm in."

"Roger that!" Doc shot back. "See you in a few hours. In the meantime, don't be surprised if you get a visitor with a briefcase."

"Why do I get the feeling there won't be cash inside?" Q chuckled.

"There's more to life than money, my friend," Doc quipped and ended the call.

As Q put his cell phone away, a black SUV stopped in front of the house and a man with a briefcase strode to the door. He gave Q a nod and handed him the case without a word. As the SUV drove off, Q opened the case on the dining room table and found a can labeled *Worms.*

"Here we go again," Q said softly as he held the can in his hand and smiled.

1

THE HATCH

Connie was thrilled with the seats she and Doc had in the front row of the first-class section of their flight to Spokane. Her plan was to sleep during most of the six-hour flight as well as the three-hour seaplane connection to Flathead Lake in Montana, so she would be rested and fresh for her house guests the next morning. But she had a change of heart while she and Doc waited to board at Washington Dulles International Airport.

"Hi Mom!" she heard a young woman say behind her. "Louis and I are waiting for our plane in D.C. We expect to land in Spokane around 1:00 a.m. Yeah, I know, Mom. But it will be worth it. I can't wait to see everyone again. How is everything going with the wedding plans? We are so excited, Mom! Louis and I can't thank you enough for handling everything for us the way you have. You're wonderful and I love you Mom! See you soon! Bye bye!"

"Sounds like your mom and dad have everything under control," Connie heard a young man say. "They've been incredible the way they've made it possible for us to quickly fly in and get married in front of family and friends before we're deployed."

Connie couldn't help herself. She turned around in her seat to see the young couple. To her great surprise, they were Marine Corps officers. The handsome young couple was all the more stunning in their Marine dress uniforms.

"Forgive me, but I couldn't help overhearing your call home," Connie said softly. "I'm so happy for the two of you. Congratulations! And thank you both for your service to the nation."

"Thank you so much!" the pretty, young sergeant replied. "My name's Jenny Charles and this is my fiancé, Master Sergeant Louis Danforth."

"I'm Connie Holiday, and I'm privileged to meet you both," Connie answered. "This is my husband, John."

"It's an honor for me, too," Doc said. "Congratulations on your upcoming wedding. Are you both from the Spokane area?"

"Just Jenny," Louis said. "We both signed up right out of college and met in the Corps. We've been together ever since."

"Semper Fi!" Doc said with a knowing smile.

"Oorah!" both Marines replied loudly and gave Doc high fives.

"I hope you two are flying first class on this memorable trip," Connie said sincerely.

"It was booked up," Jenny said sadly. "We were lucky to get seats in Coach."

"Not anymore!" Connie said, smiling at Doc and waving the first-class tickets.

"Oh, thank you, really, but," Jenny began to decline, but was cut off by Connie.

"Too late! The deal is done!" Connie said resolutely. "Hand over your tickets."

"This is incredibly kind of both of you," Louis said. "Thank you both very much."

"You both thank us every day you wake up and answer the call," Doc told him.

"Flight 1703 is now boarding first-class passengers," the announcement interrupted.

"Get going, you two," Connie told them cheerfully and watched them head to the plane.

"Well, it definitely won't be as comfortable," Connie sighed to Doc. "But I'm tired enough to sleep just about anywhere."

"You know me," Doc started to say.

"I know. I know," Connie finished his sentence for him. "Everything happens for a reason. But I have no idea what the reason was for me to swap seats. I just felt it was the right thing to do."

"I'd say that's a pretty good reason," Doc said with a smile as the general call to board came over the loudspeaker. Silently, he wondered if there might be a more ominous reason.

As Connie and Doc finally boarded, Jenny and Louis were busy telling the flight attendant their choice of beverages and which light snack they would like to hold them over until supper would be served somewhere over Minnesota.

Doc smiled, knowing his wife had such compassion and regard for members of the military. It was a side of her that first attracted him when she was his nurse at the Walter Reed National Military Medical Center two years earlier.

Doc chose a pair of seats in the last row in the tail section of the plane, put his cane and carry-on bag in the overhead compartment, and settled in with the in-flight magazine. Connie claimed the window seat. Doc was thankful no one joined them in the last row, which meant he could sit by the aisle with an empty seat between them.

As the flight attendants recited the routine emergency information, Doc lifted his armrest to take advantage of the empty center seat and squirmed into the most comfortable position possible. He was grateful for the few extra inches of room it gave him. Every inch counted because he wore his 45 caliber Wilson Combat 1911 pistol under his jacket. The

8-round semi-automatic was an emotional comfort under fire. But it would have been anything but comforting pressed against his ribcage in the cramped confines of a Coach-class seat.

He smiled as he recalled the check-in agent's look of mixed emotions when he showed his Deputy U.S. Marshal badge and ID to the gate attendant and let her know he was carrying a loaded firearm aboard with him.

"Is there a Federal Air Marshal with us on this flight?" he asked quietly.

"As a matter of fact, there isn't one, Marshal Holiday," she said as her initial look of surprise melted into calm understanding that having Doc armed on board was a good thing.

Of course, Doc hoped he wouldn't need it during the flight. But he couldn't help but wonder why Connie's act of kindness—and his choice of seats—*just happened to* put him in a position to view the entire cabin with zero effort. Looking for a distraction from that sobering thought, Doc plucked the in-flight magazine from the back of the seat in front of him with the plan to read it from cover to cover. Connie had a very different plan. She put her neck pillow on, slipped on her sleep mask, topped it all off with her sound-canceling headphones and was on her way to la-la land as the plane taxied to the runway. Both plans worked well for the first five hours of the flight.

"Excuse me, hon," Connie said to Doc as she peeled off her sleep accessories. "I have to use the bathroom."

Doc quickly unbuckled his seat belt and hopped to his feet in the aisle. Connie squeezed by, pressing against him in her wonderfully slow way, and entered the bathroom beside the galley in the tail section of the plane. As Doc settled back into his seat, his eye caught sight of a man near the front of the Coach section who had jumped to his feet and walked swiftly in the direction of First Class. Initially it didn't seem like anything more than a dash to the forward bathroom. But the man stopped abruptly at the front row and glared at Jenny and Louis. Doc saw the man say something to the couple, but didn't hear it.

"You are dogs!" the man shouted next. "Attack dogs for a government out of control!"

Two flight attendants quickly approached the man and calmly took precautionary positions: One behind him, the other between him and the Marine couple.

"Sir, we must request that you return to your seat," the attendant in front of him said.

"You are both dogs too!" the man was screaming now. "I do not take orders from dogs!"

The passengers quickly became restless and Doc calmly moved into the aisle for a clear view of the situation. The man's emotions rapidly escalated and he wheeled around and grabbed the attendant behind him by the vest. Doc knew he had to act fast. So he did.

"You are dogs too!" Doc yelled at the empty seats he and Connie had been sitting in. "You are filthy attack dogs! Your master is a war criminal and the three of you are its puppets!"

Because Doc feared that walking to First Class would escalate the man even more, he figured his best bet was to induce the man to come to him. Doc was encouraged when the man turned loose of the flight attendant's vest. He knew he had at least grabbed the man's attention. So Doc went for broke and began flailing his arms and screaming at the three empty seats. He tried to make eye contact with as many of the surrounding passengers as he could in the hope of somehow signaling to them that he was merely trying to defuse the situation.

"Sit down and shut up!" a very muscular hulk of a man shouted and rose from his seat a couple of rows ahead of Doc.

Doc was grateful the bulky passenger stood up, because the man shouting in First Class could not see past him. But Doc also feared he might lose control of the situation if it continued to escalate. To complicate things even more, he worried that Connie would exit the restroom unaware of the potentially dangerous situation unfolding in the aisle. The passengers nearest the drama in First Class all gasped as the man lunged toward Jenny and snatched a butter knife off of her supper tray. But instead of assaulting her or Louis or the flight attendants, he made a dash in Doc's direction.

The move gave Doc his first good look at the man, who stood roughly 6'3" and weighed around 200 pounds. He bore no resemblance to a radical zealot from the Middle East. Rather, the young man more closely fit the profile of a collegiate basketball player from the Midwest. For better or worse, Doc relaxed a notch or two, reasoning that he had a disturbed young man on his hands, rather than a possible suicide bomber. That didn't change the fact that the young man was now racing toward him with a butter knife clutched tightly in one hand.

"Come on! Come on!" Doc called out to the young man urgently.

But then most of the rearward passengers realized Doc must have been using the empty seats to lure the young man to the back row. But they still had no idea what was happening. They all leaned away from the aisle as the angry man rushed past. Doc figured he'd be able to disarm the man quickly enough. But he worried about doing it in such a confined space, with innocent people nearby. As the young man rushed at him, Doc committed not to pull his pistol unless it absolutely became necessary. But other than disarming the man hand-to-hand, he had no Plan B. Worse yet, the man now realized the seats Doc had been shouting at were unoccupied.

"Do you think I'm stupid?" the young man screamed at him and closed in, knife in hand.

The man slashed wildly at Doc, who instantly clamped a strong hand around the man's wrist and twisted it until the knife hit the floor. Doc had a next move, but it was thwarted when an older man in a nearby seat suddenly jumped into the fray in a rash effort to help. So the young man broke free of Doc's grip, pushed past him, and darted into the galley where there was a hatch that was only opened on the ground to clean and stock the galley between flights.

"Stop him! Don't let him open the hatch!" a flight attendant yelled, and the plane erupted in screams and passengers suddenly clogged the aisle

Just as Doc pivoted toward the galley, Connie burst out of the bathroom, nearly hitting Doc in the face with the aluminum door. Instantly, she grabbed a metal coffee pot off the galley's brewing machine and hit the young man squarely on the top of his head with it. The loud, dull THUNK it made told Doc the man would be unconscious for quite some time.

"Niiiiice worrrrk, Beauty!" Doc said with appreciation. "It was an excellent choice to use an empty pot."

"Now we know why we ended up in the back row," Connie said with a smile.

"I know you have zip ties on board somewhere," Doc said to the nearest flight attendant. "Get me a half dozen of the strongest ones you've got."

Moments later, Doc had the prisoner securely zip-tied and slouched on the toilet in the rear bathroom that Connie had just used.

"How long until we land?" Doc asked the attendant.

"Forty-five minutes," she replied.

"That will hold him," he told her. "I'll stay here with him. The galley's closed for the duration of the flight anyway, right?"

"It's almost as if you planned it that way," she said with a weary smile.

"Yeah, I was thinking the same thing," Doc said with a weary smile of his own.

"Nice work!" Louis, the Marine Master Sergeant, told him

"Not bad, I guess," Doc said while rubbing the back of his neck. "But I've lost a half step or more in my reaction time."

"So that Trident in the handle of your cane is the real thing," Louis said. "How long ago did you leave the SEALs?"

"A lifetime ago," Doc said, without elaboration.

"If you've slowed down, I wish I could have seen you in your prime," Louis said.

Standing face-to-face with Louis brought Doc's dead friend and fellow SEAL, Kenesaw Mountain Matua, to his mind.

"How tall are you?" he asked Louis.

"I'm 6'5"," Louis said.

"About 225 pounds?" Doc guessed.

"Thereabouts," Louis said with a shrug.

"Ever give any thought to becoming a SEAL?" Doc asked.

"Yeah, just a few minutes ago," Louis replied. "Well done!"

"Hey! What about me? Do I get a little credit here?" Connie asked with a nervous smile.

"I'll say! I've never seen anyone handle a coffee pot quite like you did," Louis chuckled.

"I'm just grateful it was empty, and it wasn't glass," Connie admitted.

"If you ever decide to give the SEALs a try, give me a call. I might be able to make a call or two. Who knows, it just might help simplify your application process," Doc told Louis as he handed him a calling card.

"Thanks very much, Mr. Holiday!" Louis said with interest.

"All my closest friends call me Doc," Doc said as he shook his hand. "You should too."

"Please take your seats, fasten your seatbelts, and prepare for landing," the pilot announced over the intercom.

"I would appreciate it if the four of you would remain in your seats while the police escort the suspect off the plane and the other passengers deplane," the flight attendant told them. "I'm certain the police will want to speak to the four of you about what happened."

"Of course," Doc replied and Connie and Louis nodded yes.

"I'll fill Jenny in. I'm sure she'll want to thank the two of you," Louis said, then told Connie with a smile, "Please don't share any pointers on other ways to use a coffee pot."

"I promise not to," Connie said with a laugh.

"Wait 'til I tell her we've met Doc Holiday," Louis said and headed back to his seat.

"Yeah, okay," Doc chuckled. "Just be sure to tell her I'm not the original. I'm not *that much older* than you."

2

LIMITED EDITION

When all the other passengers deplaned and two uniformed Spokane police officers took their prisoner away, Detective Abraham Malone of the Spokane PD boarded the plane, introduced himself to Doc, Connie, Jenny, and Louis, led them into a small conference room off the concourse, and took their statements.

"Start from the beginning," he said simply. "Who did the man assault first?"

"Me and my fiancé, but just verbally," Louis said. "He shouted at us over and over while we sat in our seats. We've never met him before. He was angry when he approached us. So I think our uniforms triggered him."

The rest of the story and Malone's questions took only minutes. Then he thanked both couples, waited while they re-entered the plane and retrieved their bags and Doc's cane from their overhead storage compartments, and led them back into the concourse. It had been nearly an hour since their plane landed. So the group was caught off guard when a burly, bearded man ran up to them the moment they stepped onto the concourse from the gate area.

"YOU! You got my brother arrested!" the man shouted at all of them, but was nose-to-nose with Doc, "He would never hurt anybody. He's harmless! You filthy Americans always cause trouble!"

Malone did his best to step between the man and Doc, flashed his badge, and identified himself. It did no good.

"My brother got hauled away because of you!" the burly stranger yelled and pushed Malone aside.

"Look, fella," Malone told the man. "I understand you're upset. But I gotta ask you to calm down and go home and relax. If your brother cooperates, he may be home tonight, too."

That wasn't exactly the truth, but Malone hoped to end the incident peaceably.

"Out of my way!" the man shouted at Malone and grabbed him by his necktie.

"Damn it," Malone grunted in frustration as he seized the man's wrist and twisted it, forcing the man to the floor, face down.

Malone handcuffed the man's hands behind his back and knelt with one knee in the middle of his back as he radioed airport security and informed the man of his Miranda rights. When security arrived, Malone wished Doc and his party well and sent them on their way.

"Have you reserved a rental car?" Connie asked them.

"We have," Jenny replied. "Nothing fancy, just something to get us around the short time we'll be in town."

"I really hate to say goodbye so soon after all we've been through together," Connie said, giving Doc a smile, "and we're in no great rush. How about if you ride with me in our rental to your folks' place, Jenny? Louis and John can follow us in your rental."

"I'd really enjoy that, Connie," Jenny answered enthusiastically and gave Louis a glance. "Is that okay with you, hon?"

"Sure," Louis replied with a chuckle. "I might enjoy some friendly conversation with a Navy man. I've never done that before."

"Just be careful what you ask me," Doc replied with a smile. "The Navy doesn't sugarcoat things like the Marines do."

"No fighting, boys," Connie joked. "Jenny and I will go get the Escalade I rented and wait for you to join us just before we get on the freeway. See you then. Behave."

Doc and Louis were already too busy talking to respond to Connie with more than a wave indicating they'd heard her.

"What kind of car did you reserve?" Doc asked the towering Marine.

"The cheapest mid-size they had," Louis said almost sheepishly. "We don't plan to do much driving while we're in town. So we thought we'd be practical."

"Understood," Doc simply replied as they approached the car rental counter.

"Semper fi!" the rental agent behind the counter said, and saluted Louis.

"Oorah!" Louis responded crisply with an equally crisp salute.

"Just get back, or are about to head out, Master Sergeant?" the rental agent asked.

"Getting married before heading out," Louis said with a broad grin.

"Congratulations!" the rental agent said, and shook Louis' hand over the counter. "Guess you'll be telling her Semper fi, too."

"Always do," Louis chuckled. "She's a Marine too."

"Wow! That's great!" the rental agent said with a beaming smile. "My thanks to both of you for your service."

When the rental agent finished entering Louis' information into the system, he pulled the original set of keys he'd laid on the counter and stepped into a back room. He reappeared a moment later and handed Louis a different set of keys.

"I've upgraded you," the man said with a smile. "It's a convertible. So you don't have to worry about headroom. Bring it back with an empty tank, as my gift to you both. Enjoy!"

Louis wondered what car was waiting for him and as he and Doc headed to the garage. The answer was waiting for him when they reached the check-out counter. It was a bad-ass-looking black Limited Edition Chevy Camaro ZL1 with broad, twin neon yellow racing stripes down the middle, and the top already down. It was the kind of car cops saw coming a mile away.

"Now *THIS* is the car I should have rented!" Louis said to Doc.

"You have," the young woman at the check-out desk told him, happily.

"No, I don't think so," Louis replied. "It's definitely not in the budget."

"It is now!" the woman responded. "Congratulations, Master Sergeant!"

"I don't know what to say," Louis muttered as he walked around the Camaro.

"Just say you'll bring it back on E," the woman replied.

"Roger that!" Louis called out and hit the *Start* button as Doc got in.

Louis pulled out of the garage faster than he should have. But everyone knew he would.

"Now I know why you joined the Marines," Doc said lightheartedly. "No one treats old seadogs like this."

"Believe me, Doc," Louis responded. "This is definitely out of the ordinary."

Jenny and Connie both jumped out of the Escalade when the guys pulled up in the Camaro, grinning from ear to ear.

"Louis, what have you done?!" Jenny couldn't help but ask, thinking of the cost.

"Got upgraded with no extra charge, baby!" Louis crowed. "Wait 'til you drive it!"

"Actually, I'm partial to this Escalade," Jenny cooed.

"They're both above our pay grade," Louis laughed and revved the Camaro's engine.

"No speeding, and try to stay close by, you two," Connie called out as she climbed back into the luxury Shadow Metallic SUV.

Louis eased up on the gas pedal and leisurely trailed behind the SUV by about 50 yards so he could enjoy talking with Doc. Doc opened the rental paperwork and rattled off the specs.

"6.2 Liter V8, 760 horsepower, and 720 foot-pounds of torque, Callaway SC750 supercharger package, RECARO performance bucket seats with embroidered headrests, custom wheels and brake calipers," Doc read aloud. "Man oh man, what a buggy!"

"Oorah!" Louis shouted over the sound of the wind rushing by the open sports car.

"What the heck does that mean, anyway?" Doc asked with mock irritation.

"What? Oorah?" Louis asked with mock innocence.

"Yeah," Doc said. "Aye-aye makes sense. But I can't even spell oorah."

"My father and grandfather were both submariners," Louis answered. "The way they explained it, it all started in the waters off Korea in the early 1950s among marines aboard reconnaissance subs. They imitated the alarm that sounded onboard when the subs were ordered to dive. The alarm always got their adrenalin flowing. So it became a rallying cry among them, and still is a kind of 'call to action.' My folks are both retired now and have a place down in Savannah, Georgia."

Just then, Doc's cell phone signaled a call from President Preston.

"I'm sorry, Louis," Doc said. "But this call could be important. Can you please pull over and call and ask the girls to pull over too and wait for us?"

"Sure thing," Louis said, and complied.

Doc climbed out of the Camaro and walked about ten yards along the shoulder to answer the call. Doc finally had a direct line and the formalities of the President's calls were over. As Doc punched *Answer,* he saw Connie pull the Escalade onto the shoulder about 100 yards away with her hazard lights blinking.

"Hello, Mr. President," Doc said cheerfully. "To what do I owe this honor?"

"Hello, Doc," the President said forcefully. "Are you on your way into Spokane?"

"I am," Doc answered. "But I don't like the sound of your question. What's up?"

"Something potentially very important has come up and I'm hoping you agree to fly down to Savannah, Georgia, to check it out," the President said. "We may have a very sensitive situation just off the coast—too sensitive to send the military in there asking questions. So I need someone like you to do it quietly. Is Q still at your place?"

"Yep," Doc answered simply, and marveled at the President being abreast of such details.

"Please call him and tell him to destroy the instructions he received this morning," the President said. "I've got a private plane waiting dockside at your place with new instructions onboard. If he's willing to join you, the private plane will get him to you there in Spokane. I have tickets to Savannah waiting for you both at the Spokane airport."

"I'm sure he'll be on it shortly, Mr. President," Doc assured him, and shook his head at how quickly the President could get things done. "Am I going to get wet on this trip?"

"You may," the President said cryptically.

"Well in that case, I have another fella I believe could be of great help to us down there."

"Fine, Doc, take 'em along if you think you can use him," the President said. "The ticket will be there along with yours and Q's. Gotta go, Doc. I look forward to your success. Good luck and God bless!"

"Thank you, Mr. President," Doc said. "We'll do our best and update you ASAP!"

As Doc climbed back into the Camaro, he and Louis watched a beat-up pickup truck pull onto the shoulder behind Connie and Jenny.

"Well, it looks like the girls have themselves a Good Samaritan," Louis said as he slowly rolled the Camaro up the shoulder in their direction.

As Doc and Louis approached, they saw two men exit the truck and walk to both sides of the SUV.

"Now that's odd," Doc said slowly, sizing-up the scene.

He was grateful Connie always locked the doors when she drove, and he hoped he was beginning to worry for no good reason. Louis brought the Camaro to a slow roll near the truck.

"Pull up in front of the Escalade, please, Louis," Doc said.

Louis whipped the black muscle car around in front of the SUV in a flash.

"Mighty nice car you got there boys," the guy on Connie's side of the SUV said as Louis and Doc climbed out onto the shoulder. "And that's a mighty fancy uniform you have on, son. But we got this under control. So you can keep right on rollin' down the road."

"The car's a rental. I'm not your son...and you are

both officially relieved," Louis said coolly, but firmly. "Thank you for your selfless act of kindness, gentlemen. Have a nice day and a safe trip."

Louis walked to the driver's side of the Escalade. Doc grabbed his cane from the back seat of the Camaro and walked to the passenger side of the SUV. He knew the look on Connie's face. The men they'd walked up on had obviously said something that upset her and she had lost patience with them.

"Maybe you didn't hear me," the man on Connie's side of the SUV said to Louis, who towered over him. "I said we got this under control. Now move on, before I mess up that pretty uniform of yours!"

Doc was in awe of the man's stupidity. He couldn't wait to see how Louis responded.

"Are you and Jenny alright, Connie?" Louis asked through the partially open window.

"We're fine," Connie answered, "just very annoyed!"

"So you all know each other," the man said to Louis. "Ain't this cozy?"

"Just move on and simplify things for us all," Louis said, giving the man one last chance.

But the mouthy man instead took a wild swing. Louis grasped the man's fist in his huge right hand, grabbed him around the throat with his left hand, lifted him off the ground, and pressed him against the rear door of the Escalade, then stepped in close between his legs to avoid being kicked. It was a move Doc had only seen one other man make...his late best friend, Mountain. The memory distracted Doc just long enough for the man on the passenger side to think he could get the drop on him.

"Whoa, big daddy!" Doc said as he calmly lifted the left side of his jacket just enough for the man to see the handle of his 1911. "I only pull this if I intend to use it... and I'm real close to pulling it. So now's a good time for you to convince your partner it's time to go."

"Let's go, Dwight!" the man shouted to the guy Louis had just lowered to the ground.

For a moment, it sounded as though their truck wasn't going to start. But everyone relaxed when the engine came to life and Dwight burnt rubber getting back onto the highway.

"Dwight?" Louis chuckled. "Who names their kid Dwight?"

"The Eisenhowers," Doc laughed in response.

"*Besides them*," Louis said in agitation.

"The Yoakams," Jenny said with a giggle.

"Okay, point made," Louis sighed.

Five more minutes down the road, Doc thought he'd better bring up the Savannah trip before he ran out of time.

"Hey, Louis," Doc began, "didn't you say your folks live in Savannah?"

"Yep," he answered. "Been there nearly 20 years now. I lived there most of my life."

"How well do you know the coastal area?" Doc asked.

"*VERY* well!" Louis shot back. "Tybee Island was my second home during high school."

"I don't have the details yet," Doc said, "but our government has asked me to go to the Georgia coast to ask some questions, and you could be a big help. We'll only be gone a couple of days and I can guarantee Jenny you'll be back in plenty of time for the wedding. Do you think you might be able to do that?"

"When you say, 'our government,' who exactly do you mean?" Louis asked, knowing the probable answer.

"A senior government official," Doc said in the hope it provided the leverage he needed.

"Well…" Louis hesitated.

"I could really use your knowledge and experience down there," Doc added for effect. "And you never know just how grateful that senior government official might be."

"I do want to help…" Louis admitted.

"C'mon, Louis," Doc reasoned. "You've got six whole days before the wedding. I'll have you back here in your future in-laws' house in no more than four days. What do you say?"

"Well, you gotta give me a few minutes alone with Jenny before I commit to anything," Louis sighed. "Why did this have to come up now, of all times?"

"Because you're here, that's why. And like I always say, everything happens for a reason," Doc said cheerfully and gave Louis a high five just two miles before their exit. "By the way," Doc added, "you *do* have a security clearance *don't you*?"

"Hi, Mom!" Jenny excitedly said into her cell phone when her mom's phone went to call waiting. "We're only ten minutes away! Can't wait to hug you both! Sorry I didn't give you more notice, but I've brought a couple friends along unexpectedly. So I'll prepare another bedroom once we get settled in. I love you! See you in a few minutes!"

3

THIS WOULD NOT BE THE DAY

I n Montana, Q got Doc's text telling him to expect another can of "worms" to destroy the earlier can, and start packing a bag for a two- to three-day trip to the Georgia Coast.

"**i really need you, Q or i would have sent this in the form of a request**

i promise to ask nicely next time ... if i can."

As Q texted his reply from the Holidays' front porch and contemplated how to break it to Marsha, he caught sight of another hulking black Suburban approaching via the dock area below.

"Let me guess," his wife, Marsha, sighed. "Here comes another can of worms and the last one hasn't even been opened yet."

"It expired on the shelf," Q said, trying to lighten the moment.

"How long will you be gone this time?" she asked her husband.

"Two or three days, tops," Q quickly answered hopefully. "In the meantime, you get to enjoy some time with Connie after all. By the way, have you seen Noah and Madeleine lately?"

"They went for a walk down by the lake," Marsha said.

Q picked up the binoculars he found beside the porch swing and scanned the shore below. He spotted the couple about a half mile away, headed back. His first thought was to call Noah. But he knew what Noah would say. So he texted Doc back to tell him Noah was coming too.

Doc, in turn, texted "4" to the number the President had given him for text messages a while back. He knew the President would understand and arrange for four tickets to Savannah.

Moments later, Connie pulled the Escalade to the curb in front of a classic middle-class bungalow with a perfectly manicured front yard. Louis parked the Camaro in the driveway and the couples converged on the front porch.

"JENNY!" the woman who was obviously her mother yelled, and hugged her tightly.

"We've missed you so," her obvious father told her and took his turn hugging her.

"I've missed you both terribly," Jenny said while hugging back. "I'm so glad to be home!"

After the introductions, Louis grabbed their largest suitcases and followed Jenny and her mom into the bedroom they'd use for the week. When Jenny's mom returned to the living room to lead Doc and Connie to their room, Louis closed the bedroom door and broke the news.

"Jenny, Mr. Holiday's asked me to make a quick trip down to Savannah, Georgia, with him on what he says is important government business," he said in one breath.

"What?" Jenny said with understandable confusion. "We're here to get married, Louis. Why would you take off with someone we only just met and go all the way down to Georgia? I thought you were going to spend time getting to know my parents better."

"I definitely will, Jenny," Louis promised. "I'll still have a lot of time when I get back. He got an urgent call from Washington during the ride from the airport. That's why we had to pull over. I don't know the details yet, but I know the reason is important and I'd already mentioned to Mr. Holiday that I have family in Savannah. He's got to go down to Tybee Island and ask folks some questions, and he asked me to go because I know the area."

"I don't like the idea of you being gone, Louis," she said. "We only have so much time together before we ship out. Mr. Holiday's military, but retired. Is he law enforcement?"

"I'm not sure," Louis admitted. "But I know he carries a gun and he's well connected."

"Well, I know you want to go," Jenny said. "And you can see your folks, too."

"Thanks honey," Louis said sincerely. "I'll be back before you miss me!"

"I know that's not true," she cooed. "Just get back here as soon as you can."

Louis carried his suitcase back outside to the

Escalade. Doc was close behind and opened the doors remotely.

"You can't wear your uniform for this mission, Louis," Doc said. "The more we blend in down there, the better. Do you have a side arm with you?"

"I don't," Louis replied with a puzzled look on his face. "What am I getting into, Mr. Holiday? I thought we were just going to ask some questions."

"I just always make a point of knowing what firepower's available," Doc answered, hoping to reassure Louis of his safety. "Old habits die hard, I guess. We are just going there to get some answers. So you can be sure we're not going to do anything to make folks nervous. As a matter of fact, the point is to get in and get out with as few interactions as possible."

As Doc and Louis headed back to the house, Jenny's father stepped out onto the porch.

"Leaving already, Louis?" he called out with a smile. "Was it something I said, or are you just getting cold feet?"

"No, the wedding's still on, Mr. Charles," Louis laughed. "But something's come up and Mr. Holiday and I have to spend a day or two in Savannah, Georgia. I'm sorry to rush off like this, but at least I'll have a bit of time with my folks while I'm there."

"I'm just yankin' your chain, son," Mr. Charles said with a grin and led the guys back into the house.

"Jenny tells me you're a retired Navy man too," he said to Doc in the living room.

"I am," Doc said. "Almost three years already."

"Where'd you serve most of your time?" Mr. Charles asked.

"All over the world, really," Doc said, "with the SEALs."

"Really?" Mr. Charles said with a knowing smile. "So you saw some action, I suspect."

"A bit, sir," Doc said simply. "A bit."

"Well, I was hoping we could swap some stories, but now I know that's not going to happen," Mr. Charles chuckled.

"When we get back, I'd appreciate hearing some of yours," Doc told him.

When the women walked into the living room, Doc quietly took Connie out to the porch.

"The President's asked me to fly down to Savannah, Georgia, to ask some folks a few questions," he told her. "But I'll be back in a couple of days. I promise."

"Doc, this is unfair," Connie said. "We're not even home yet and you're leaving again."

"I hear you, Beauty," Doc agreed. "But the President says it's urgent."

"When you're the President, *everything is urgent*," she said.

"You have a point," Doc agreed again. "I promise I'll be back in a day or two. Q and Noah are headed this way in a small charter plane. You could catch it for the return trip to Flathead and enjoy a couple of quiet days with Marsha and Madeleine."

"That sounds like a good idea," Connie admitted. "We may even have a girls' night out."

"After this trip, you're due for one," Doc agreed.

After a quick supper and long goodbye hugs with Jenny and her parents, Doc, Connie, and Louis climbed into the Escalade and headed to the airport to rendezvous with Q and Noah. Connie filled the short ride to the airport with small talk about how she would be glad to get home and what she and Marsha and Madeleine might do with the time they'd have together.

The tenor of Connie's voice told Doc she was worried. He was too. But when they wed, they made a pact not to dwell on worries about the missions. The day that one or the other of them could no longer do that would be the day Doc would retire. But this would not be the day.

Doc pulled the Escalade up to a security gate at the edge of the airport and showed the guard his ID.

"We're meeting a small private plane on Runway 7," Doc told the guard. "It's due in minutes and we'll be gone right after it lands."

"Very good," the guard simply said and waved them through.

The plane arrived right on time and the team—plus one—was together again. Noah and Q hopped out with their bags. Louis loaded Connie's bags onto the plane while she and Doc said goodbye to one another.

"I'll be back the moment I can be, Beauty," Doc told Connie as he took her in his arms.

"I'll miss you, my love," Connie said as she held Doc a little longer and a little tighter than usual. "Come home to me safe and sound. Do you hear me?"

"Aye-aye!" Doc said crisply and hugged her tightly during their goodbye kiss. "You are my sunshine, Beauty!"

Connie climbed aboard the seaplane and said a silent prayer for Doc and his partners as

the plane took off for its return trip to Flathead Lake, where Marsha and Madeleine eagerly awaited her return.

Q handed Doc the new can of "worms" and he opened it with his Schrade SC90.

"That's quite a blade you have there, Mr. Holiday," Louis said.

"I never leave home without it," Doc said as he pried the can open and pulled out the document it contained. "And call me Doc, would you please?"

"Okay, Doc," Louis simply replied a little defensively.

"Don't let him intimidate you, Louis," Q said. "Just let him growl. It works for us."

"I'll remember that," Louis answered.

"What do the 'worms' say?" Noah asked as Doc unfolded the document.

"The President thinks radicals may have located the Tybee Island H-Bomb," Doc said.

"You're kidding, right?!" Louis blurted out. "The President actually believes that story? I've listened to that crap about the Tybee Bomb most of my life. I've still got Tybee Island Bomb Squad t-shirts in my old room at my folks' house, for God's sake. This is ridiculous!"

"What are you two talking about?" Noah asked

"In February 1958, a B-47 Bomber was headed to Homestead Air Force Base, south of Miami, after completing a training exercise." Doc read the opening to the document aloud. "Approximately seven miles off the coast of Georgia, east of Tybee Island, near the mouth of the Savannah River, an F-86 Fighter Jet participating in the exercise somehow collided with the B-47 and crippled it 38,000 feet in the air. To maintain enough altitude to make it to Hunter Air Force Base, outside of Savannah, the pilot dropped the Mark 15 class hydrogen bomb over the ocean."

"Seriously?!" Noah interrupted. "A live hydrogen bomb?! What happened?!"

"Nothing," Doc said simply. "The Air Force has never admitted the bomb was armed. So researchers still disagree on whether or not the bomb's plutonium nuclear core had been installed during the flight. If it had, the bomb was—and still is—fully functional."

"That can't be good!" Q stated the obvious.

"How big is it?" Louis asked anxiously.

"A Mark 15 bomb is twelve feet long, three feet wide, weighs nearly eight tons, plus 400 pounds of conventional high explosives and an unknown amount of highly enriched uranium."

"That's the size of a large cargo van," Louis guessed. "And it's 100 times more powerful than the Hiroshima bomb," he added from memory.

"And you're telling us that bomb was never retrieved?" Q asked, hoping he was wrong.

"The Air Force and Navy couldn't find it," Doc answered. "They think the bomb is at least 15 feet deep in the mud, under 100 or more feet of water."

"They looked for it for weeks," Louis added. "But the hunt attracted so much attention folks along the beaches got pretty nervous. Residents and tourists demanded to know if it was safe to be on the coast. Meanwhile, the Air

Force concluded the crew had not armed the bomb during the flight. So they decided to cut bait and let the bomb stay wherever it landed."

"According to this info, the bomb would pose a huge risk in the wrong hands. The uranium onboard can make water all along the east coast undrinkable. In the worst-case scenario, terrorists would have the makings of a dirty bomb that could unleash fatal radiation poisoning in a 100-mile radius."

"And radicals are now looking for it," Q said, "which means we have to find it first."

"The President fears they may have already found it," Doc said.

"If so, we have to find them before they figure out how to retrieve it," Q concluded.

"Roger that!" Doc said, as he tucked the coordinates into a leg pocket of his cargo pants, set the rest of the document on fire in the can, and said, "Let's do this team!"

Just minutes later, Doc parked the SUV in the *Long Term* lot and the team unloaded their luggage. During the shuttle ride to the terminal, Doc began to wonder how big a network the radicals might have, how well-funded they were, and what their ultimate objective might be.

Finding and retrieving a hydrogen bomb that had been lost for more than 70 years had to be a difficult and expensive proposition. The coordinates might indicate they'd found it, but as far as the President knew, they hadn't yet retrieved it. Was that because of the difficulty of the task—or the immense difficulty of doing it secretly? Doc didn't entertain the thought of what the radicals intended to do with the bomb. Whatever their intention, Doc was sure it wasn't good.

That dark thought kicked the door of Doc's imagination wide open, unleashing memories of how bloodthirsty radicals of missions past had been. He was struggling to get that horrific door in his mind closed again when Louis moved into the seat beside him at the rear of the shuttle.

"So what's the plan, Doc?" Louis asked quietly.

"Don't really have one yet," Doc admitted. "But for starters, I think the four of us should travel as strangers. Showing up as a group could attract attention. So we'll check our bags separately and act like we don't know one another on the plane. I know you'll stay at your folks' place. Before we board, I'll reserve separate hotels for the rest of us and four rental cars."

"Do you really think that's necessary?" Louis asked innocently.

"I don't really know, Louis," Doc answered honestly. "There's a lot I don't know about this mission. That typically brings surprises. So it's always wise to bring some surprises of our own along with us. That's the one thing *I do know*."

"Well, I'd better call my folks with an update, because they're no doubt getting ready to fly to Spokane for the wedding," Louis said. "What should I tell them about why I'm coming home?"

"You can tell 'em it's official business," Doc said. "But don't share any details just yet."

"That'll be easy," Louis replied. "I don't have any details."

Louis knew his father would accept the official business explanation, but he worried it might leave his mother concerned for his safety. So he planned to keep things light at home.

4

SMALL, QUIET, AND INCONSPICUOUS

Noah had told the team his folks lived in Savannah. That wasn't exactly true. They actually had a beautiful oceanfront home on Skidaway Island. They named it Sugar Tree, in honor of the tall, thick sugarberry trees that stood between the house and the ocean. The bright white mini-mansion had six bedrooms, six and a half baths, and a huge second floor sun deck that spanned the rear of the home and rose above the sugarberry trees, providing a breathtaking view of the ocean—and Tybee Island to the northeast.

Louis arrived at Sugar Tree first and briefly explained why the others would arrive roughly twenty minutes apart. His father had seen enough action in the Navy to not need many details. Louis handled the introductions as each member of the team arrived. Once they all arrived, his mother, Sherryl, showed them their rooms and served a quick brunch of steak, eggs, potatoes, and biscuits with sausage gravy.

"So, Mr. Danforth, how is it you're not at least 600 pounds?" Doc asked with a laugh.

"I get a lot of exercise," Louis' dad replied with his own hardy laugh. "And please call me Jim. 'Mr. Danforth' makes me feel old enough to be my own father."

"Between his business and just being out on one of his boats, he's always on the go," Sherryl laughed. "Sometimes it feels like he's still serving aboard those nuke submarines."

"You were a submariner?" Doc asked. "That could be tough duty."

"Yeah, but I think some of those six-month deployments gave the wife just enough of a break that she was able to put up with me when I was home," Jim laughed.

"So what line of work are you fellas in?" Jim asked.

"I'm a U.S. Marshal," Q answered before Doc could make something up. "I'm down here on assignment and I've deputized this sorry bunch because I couldn't trust 'em enough to leave 'em behind. That doesn't apply to your son Louis, here," Q said, patting Louis on the back. "I brought him along as a guide. We expect to be gone in a couple of days."

"Just don't get our boy shot," Jim said half-kidding. "It's bad enough we got to deal with him shipping out to the Middle East in a week and a half. I don't want to think the government would put in him harm's way here at home."

"He's in the best of hands, Jim," Doc said reassuringly. "I promise you we'll take good care of him, Mrs. Danforth," he softly said to Louis' mother.

"You better!" she answered abruptly. "He's the best part of what Jim and I have worked all our lives for, and I plan to dance at his wedding this weekend."

Her answer reawakened Doc to the reality of the short amount of time they had available to find out what they could. And the team had to get to work.

"Now, if you fellas are done eatin' and jawin', follow me up to the sun deck," Jim said. "You can get a pretty good lay of the land and sea from up there."

Jim stopped just inside the door that led to the sun deck and withdrew a handsome Arturo Fuente Opus X BBMF cigar from a large teak wood humidor.

"Anyone else care for one?" he asked and waved his in the air.

"Since you're offering!" Q said excitedly.

"You know I want one," Louis replied with an outstretched hand.

Cigars in hand, Jim led the men onto an expansive, hardwood deck overlooking the Atlantic in the midday sun.

Doc walked to the railing while Jim pulled out a brushed chrome Zippo lighter with a brass U.S. Navy Anchor emblem and lit the smokes.

"Wow! You weren't exaggerating," Doc said appreciatively as he surveyed the view. "Retirement's been good to you I see!"

"No complaints," Jim agreed and put an arm around Louis' shoulders. "I'm a blessed man in many ways. It's good to have you home, Son," he told Louis quietly, "even if it's only for a couple of days."

"Is that Tybee Island?" Q asked and pointed northeast.

"It is," Jim confirmed.

"You obviously aren't concerned about the missing H-bomb," Noah guessed.

"Not really," Jim said matter-of-factly. "But to tell you the truth, I do make a point of keeping an eye on the water in the general vicinity—such as we know it."

"Where's that?" Doc asked as he stepped in next to Jim.

"Right out there," Jim said and pointed. "It's approximately a 12-square-mile area, which I think is why folks around here hardly give it a thought. Logic says the military would have found it one way or another by now if it really posed a threat."

Doc cast his eyes down at the deck and answered, "It's not often you hear the words 'logic' and 'military' in the same sentence."

"If they're wrong, it'll wreak havoc on your property value," Q joked.

"If they're wrong," Jim added, "Sherryl and I won't be around long enough to worry about our property value."

"Right or wrong, Jim," Doc said, "we're here to find out if someone besides the military is looking for it...or have maybe found it already."

"And what if they have?" Jim asked.

"That, I can't tell you," Doc replied. "My best guess is that the Navy's got a ship nearby, likely a submarine with salvage technology to snatch the bomb off the bottom. That part is way above my pay grade. After all, I'm officially retired. Remember?"

"You sure have a funny way of spending your retirement," Jim laughed. "I suppose you're going to need a boat while you're here, aren't ya'?"

"That would be helpful, yes," Doc said. "Something small, quiet, and inconspicuous."

"I can make that happen," Jim said. "But a boat that accommodates the five of us won't exactly be what I would call small."

"Whoa!" Doc said abruptly. "I'm sorry, but you can't be involved in this, Jim. We're acting on official orders from Washington and they don't include you."

"Well, then maybe they don't include my boat either," Jim huffed and bluffed.

"Dad, I know you understand the situation," Louis said gently. "This is a sensitive, classified matter. We have explicit orders not to involve 'locals' unless it's absolutely necessary."

"Well, what if I say it's 'absolutely necessary'?" Jim tried to hold his ground.

"Do you?" Doc called him on it.

"No, I guess not," Jim sighed. "Sherryl wouldn't okay it even if the government did."

"Sorry Dad, really," Louis said and gave his father a side hug.

"Okay guys," Jim said boldly. "I know you have to get going and so do I. Who's going with me to the marina?"

"That would be me," Doc replied. "Fellas I need you to canvas the island as quietly as you can. Try to find out if outsiders are down here snooping around."

Noah, Q, and Louis climbed into their cars and headed toward Tybee Island. Doc hopped into Jim's

Grand Cherokee for the short ride to Jim's *Sea Me Marina,* where Jim hooked him up with a 24-foot Sea Fox Chief fishing boat.

"All you need to do is enter the coordinates into the navigation system and this baby will take you exactly where you want to go," Jim proudly told him. "Are you sure I can't come along?" Jim tried to join in one last time.

"Sorry, Jim," Doc replied. "There's just too many unknowns."

"Well, it's a great afternoon to be on the water," Jim relented. "So take care of yourself out there and try to have a good time."

"Aye-aye!" Doc said crisply and started the twin engines while Jim undid the mooring lines, then watched Doc hit the throttle and send the boat out to sea.

Doc felt bad about not taking Jim along. He really didn't expect any danger on this jaunt, and knowing Jim was a former submariner made it clear the old seadog could keep secrets. But as he'd told Jim, there were just too many unknowns to involve him unnecessarily.

Heading out on the open sea brought Doc's nervous system alive. The sun was shining and the water was calm. There were just enough other boats on the water to ensure his didn't attract attention. He purposely didn't enter the coordinates right away, so it wouldn't appear he was going there deliberately.

"This is a wonderful day!" Doc sang out in his brain. "I need to do more of this! I wish Connie was here to enjoy this with me!"

Doc's next thought was how terrific it was that

cruising aimlessly for a while was the best thing he could do to disguise his objective. So that's exactly what he did for the next two hours.

Meanwhile, Q walked into the local hardware store and just browsed until the owner approached him.

"Can I help you find something?" the white-haired man with a lot of mustache and a slight limp asked him.

If you only knew, Q thought to himself.

"Actually, I'm just killing time while my wife shops at the dress shop across the street. But now that you've asked, I do need to have some keys made."

Q figured he could always use extra house and car keys, and getting new ones cut would give him some time to ask questions.

"Be happy to do it!" the owner answered and led the way to the key cutting machine. "How many do you have?"

"Well, I need a new set of keys for my old Ford pick-up back home, and a couple of house keys for my place and two rental properties," Q made it up as he went along.

"So where's home?" the owner asked while he set the first key in place.

"Oh, I live in Frederick, Maryland," Q said. "I'm just out here for a couple of days of sun and sea. You probably get a lot of folks down here for the same reason."

"You bet we do," the owner answered and cut the first key.

"Bet you get all kinds through here, too," Q began fishing for info.

"YOU BET WE DO!" the owner laughed and set the second key for copying.

"Have you had any in here lately who just kinda stuck out as different?" Q asked.

"Not really," the owner answered, "Why do you ask?"

"No reason," Q replied. "Just makin' small talk."

"So why didn't you have these keys cut in D.C.?" the owner asked as he set the second key for cutting.

"Like I said," Q answered, "I'm just killin' time while the wife shops across the street."

Q ended the small talk and the owner quickly cut the other two keys, rang them up, and sent Q on his way. Just in case the owner watched where he went once he left the hardware store, Q walked into the dress shop across the street.

"Can I help you with anything, handsome?!" the well-dressed and over-perfumed, 50-something saleslady asked him with her best smile.

"N-no, ma'am," Q stuttered. "I'm lookin' for my wife. She said she needed a dress while we're in town. Have you had a good-looking brunette about your height in here in recently?"

"You're the only good-looking customer I've had in here all day," she answered coyly.

"Well, I guess I better keep movin' if I'm going to catch up with her," Q replied and bumped into a rack of dresses as he backed toward the door.

"If you don't find her, come on back and see me," the saleslady called to him. "I'll keep her here if she wanders in, okay?"

"O-o-kay!" Q said as he stepped outside.

"You're a pitiful old man," Q told himself. "How could a woman in her 50s set you back on your heels so easy? You have a harder time facing friendly women than angry men."

Q figured his next move ought to be to simply cruise about the island and keep an eye out for a group of men who looked like outsiders.

Noah tagged along with Louis to the Tybee Island Marina to say hello to Tony, the owner, and ask what boats he'd rented out recently.

"Louis!" Tony shouted when he saw the young Marine walk in the door. "What a great surprise! I heard you're shipping out next week, but I didn't know you were going to be home first. In fact...aren't you supposed to be getting married too?"

"Yes, on all counts," Louis said with a firm handshake. "I got a chance to visit and I jumped on it. This is my friend, Noah Hightower, Tony."

"Well, it's great to see you, Son!" Tony said with a broad smile. "And I'm pleased to meet you Mr. High-tower. What brings the two of you in?"

"I'm wondering what boats you've rented in the past couple of weeks," Louis answered.

"Let's take a look at the system," Tony said and led the way to the counter.

"It's awful quiet in here right now, Tony. How's business been?" Louis asked.

"Pretty good actually," Tony replied as he punched the keys on his computer. "As a matter of fact, we turned a guy away last week because we didn't have a boat fast enough to suit him."

"He wasn't happy with that Hydra Sports 4200 Siesta of yours?" Louis asked.

"It's not available," Tony said. "I had a group of guys rent it for two solid weeks and it's not due back for another couple of days."

"Interesting," Louis said and perked up. "How'd they pay for it?"

"Well, they gave me a cash deposit, and I wasn't about to turn down a two-week rental."

"You didn't ask for a credit card?" Louis asked, surprised.

"They said they didn't have one." Tony shrugged. "Business isn't so good that I'll turn down a wad of cash. The guy who signed for it had a bankroll as big as my fist."

"You did get a copy of his driver's license and the address he's staying at here on the island, didn't you?"

"Of course I did," Tony said, irritated now. "What's it to you, Louis?"

"I'm down here on special assignment, looking for oddball outsiders," Louis said. "Sounds like they may fit the bill. Can you please trust me enough to give me the fella's info?"

"I guess it won't hurt nothin'," Tony said and hit *Print*. "But I don't want any trouble."

"I promise there won't be," Louis said, and hoped he was right.

Louis and Noah exited the marina minutes later and headed for the motel where the mystery man claimed to be staying.

By that time a storm was blowing in from the east.

The water was getting choppy and the horizon was dark with big, dark, heavy clouds that were closing in fast. Doc was about twelve miles off shore; well beyond the coordinates he'd been given. So he turned around and headed back toward Tybee Island...right into the path of the men he sought.

5

THE "THUNDER CHILD"

"Hello!" Doc said out loud as he approached the coordinates the President had sent him and he spotted some sort of activity aboard a boat that was dead in the water. Doc ignored the growing whitecaps rocking the boat and turned off the motor, then climbed atop its broad canopy for a better look with his binoculars. The boat rocked so much Doc had to hold onto a railing with one hand as he watched three men move about their boat and lower something over the side. But distance and the rocking of the boat made it impossible to know what it was.

"What are you hombres up to?" Doc quietly asked out loud.

He was sure the men were up to something. With water so rough, casual boaters would have headed to shore already. These were no casual boaters. One appeared to be wearing a full motorcycle-type helmet, which Doc thought was extremely odd out on the open sea. So he recorded video through his binoculars, and hoped the Navy could enhance the images. Doc suddenly caught sight of a guy on the other boat looking back at him with binoculars of his own. The whipping wind made it impossible to hear what the man shouted, but Doc saw him point in his direction as the others scrambled to retrieve whatever it was they had lowered over the side. The waves were rocking and rolling by then and Doc nearly lost his grip as he climbed down from the canopy.

Doc knew he'd made a dumb mistake going out on the sea alone. But he didn't have time to regret it. As he slipped back into the captain's chair at the controls, he saw the other boat head his way at high speed. His gut told him not to pretend to be an innocent boater and let the men pull alongside him. So he turned his Sea Fox out to sea and pushed the throttle all the way open. The boat bounced so violently as it cut into the waves Doc had to stand up at the controls and grip the wheel with both hands. He suddenly wished he had let Louis' father come along.

Back at the Sea Me Marina, Jim struggled with the bystander role he'd accepted. While his son Doc and the others were on a mission for the country he'd spent a career faithfully serving, he sat passively behind the counter, resting on his elbows, tapping his fingers on the countertop. He gave it his best effort, opened the latest copy of *Salt Water Sportsman* magazine, and tried to find an interesting article. It didn't work.

With the storm blowing in and his patience completely gone, Jim convinced himself Doc would need a hand out on the open water if the waves got any higher.

So he hustled to the rooftop observation tower and scanned the water through his binoculars. It gave him an eagle-eye view of the black clouds and lightning growing on the horizon, and there was no sign of Doc.

"Damned fool!" Jim muttered under his breath, all too familiar with sailors' boldness.

Jim hustled back down to the front office, put the *Closed* sign in the window, locked the front door, and headed into the cavernous hanger where he stored his customers' more expensive boats. He was headed to the *Thunder Child*, a state-of-the-art interceptor-type craft.

It belonged to J.W. Brown, a Boston-based billionaire entrepreneur and the first customer Jim ever had. J.W. made his fortune speculating in startups and takeovers. His most recent investment in a shipbuilder landed him the *Thunder Child.* Created for military naval interceptions and drug enforcement applications, the blade-shaped, gun-metal gray power boat was unlike any Jim—or anyone else—had ever seen before.

The sleek, stealthy-looking, 60-foot, wave-slicing, fiberglass rocket displaced 20 tons, with a draft of just two feet, nine inches. Its 1,320-gallon fuel tank gave it a 750-mile range, powered by twin Caterpillar C12.9 1,000 hp diesel engines. Best of all...it was moored in the marina's enclosed boat well, fueled and ready to go at any time. For Jim, the time was now!

"Hi, J.W.!" Jim said cheerfully into his cell phone. "How ya' doin' today?"

"I'm fine, Jim," J.W. said slowly. "What a surprise. I

was just thinking about you and how we haven't talked in a while."

"Well, J.W.," Jim drawled, "you know I've never asked you for a favor before, but things are kinda slow around here this week and I have a lot of time on my hands. So I was thinkin' about how I have your beautiful boat, the *Thunder Child*, tied up and fueled with nowhere to go. And I'm wondering if it might be possible to take her out for a short cruise up the coast and back. It's a mighty beautiful craft, J.W. And it's a shame to see her idle week after week while you're up there in Beantown, ignoring her, cause you're busy making money."

"So my *Thunder Child* has seduced you, has she?" J.W. chuckled into the phone. "Well, she's probably as ready for some action as you are, and I can't get down there for at least another month. So you might be doing both me and her a favor."

"Thanks, J.W.," Jim said with a huge grin. "I owe you one."

"You owe me at least two." J.W. chuckled some more. "You take good care' of her. Ya hear me? She's unlike anything you've ever run your hands over and she's enough boat for two men at least. So you might want a copilot along for the ride."

"I know just the guy," Jim replied. "Thanks, J.W. Be well and I'll see you soon."

"You bet, good friend. Goodbye," J.W. said and ended the call.

Doc sprinted to the *OPEN* button and the double doors slid apart, revealing the angry ocean beyond. Pelting rain and a loud thunderclap split the air just as

Jim pulled *Thunder Child* out of the hanger, into the very wind, rain, and lightning she was designed to laugh at.

"Okay, baby," Jim said softly as he throttled her up. "Let's see what you're made of!"

Fifty yards from shore, Jim eased the throttle forward and *Thunder Child's* twin diesels below deck roared and rumbled their approval. It threw Jim back in his high-back captain's chair and he wisely tightened his safety harness.

"Whoa, baby!" Jim hollered. "You're more than I even dreamed you were!"

Thunder Child sliced through waves that would have capsized lesser boats her size at the speed she was traveling. At fifty knots, Doc had to literally clench his teeth to keep them from banging together as the mighty boat pounded its way forward. Thankfully, Doc had given Jim the coordinates before setting out alone earlier. Jim slowed the ship just enough to let go of the controls and set the coordinates. Then he throttled back up to 50 knots and was on the rescue mission of his life.

Meanwhile, Doc was in deep trouble. A quick look over his shoulder made it clear the suspect boat was gaining on him fast. He couldn't possibly outrun it and the violent water made outmaneuvering them impossible. He suddenly heard a hard impact in the fiberglass hull of the boat and realized he was being shot at. At just 30 knots, he was a sitting duck.

Another loud impact rang out, much closer to Doc this time, and he knew he made an easy target standing at the controls. In desperation, Doc shut the 300 horse-power Mercury SeaPro off, hit the deck, and drew his

PT111 pistol. He knew the .45 mm was no match for the firepower of the men chasing him. But he had eight rounds and he intended to make them count.

As his boat rocked wildly in the rain and unforgiving waves, Doc got a look over the side and got his first close look at the men as the cruiser circled him about 50 yards out. The one with the rifle was about to fire off another round, but stopped as his boat suddenly turned out to sea.

What the hell is that all about? Doc thought, and was able to breathe again.

Just then, Doc heard an approaching roar unlike anything he'd heard on the water before. Off the stern, he saw a strange-looking craft approach at a speed that didn't seem possible for its size and the size of the waves. It literally cut through the water like a hot knife through butter.

Doc still couldn't believe the look and power of the craft as it pulled alongside.

The sinister-looking vessel had a fully enclosed cabin with blacked-out windows and *Thunder Child – SV17* painted on the side. It stopped suddenly, dead in the water, and almost silent alongside Doc's boat. He hoped it was the Coast Guard. But then the hatch flew open and Jim jumped on deck with a 12-foot boat hook.

"Drop the anchor on that bucket. Then grab this pole and get your ass aboard!" Jim shouted over the storm.

Doc did as he was told and Jim literally yanked him aboard and pulled him into the cabin.

"Thank God you showed up, Jim!" Doc said, thinking they would head for shore.

"Let's see exactly what the *Thunder Child* can do!" Jim shouted with a smile and turned in the direction of the other boat.

Doc hated the idea of Jim getting involved. But it was obviously too late to avoid it.

"Buckle up, grab somethin', and hold on!" Jim said as he pushed the throttle completely open and Doc fell into a bucket seat.

"There's no way we'll catch 'em in this storm," Doc shouted over the rumbling thunder.

"Don't be too sure of that!" Jim shouted back.

"We don't have enough firepower if we *do* catch 'em," Doc shouted.

"Might not need it!" Jim shouted in turn.

The waves had swelled to five feet high, but the *Thunder Child* handled them like nothing Doc had experienced before.

"Ain't this bucket somethin'!" Jim shouted admiringly. "Wooo Hooo!" he whooped as they raced out to sea at what Doc knew had to be close to 70 knots.

This isn't possible, Doc thought to himself, but was glad he was wrong.

Thunder Child had no trouble catching up with the men they were after. As they gained on the cabin cruiser, it was obvious the men on board were in serious trouble. The boat was listing and nearly swamped, but the guy at the controls was recklessly pushing the craft on, into the pounding, punishing waves that threatened to break it apart.

Jim slowed *Thunder Child* about 100 feet off their port

bow and watched all three men struggle to stay on their feet and not be thrown into the raging sea.

"Don't get too close, Jim," Doc warned him. "They've got at least one rifle onboard and already shot at me!"

"Nothin' to worry about, Doc," Jim said confidently. "They can hardly stay on their feet. They sure can't aim a rifle."

No sooner had Jim said that, that one of the men grabbed a rifle and tried to aim it.

"Hang on to somethin'!" Jim shouted and pushed the throttle completely open again.

As *Thunder Child* roared to life, Jim whipped it in a tight circle around the rust bucket cabin cruiser, with ease. As he did, a giant wave caught it and rolled it over, bottom-up, leaving Jim and Doc hanging in their safety harnesses for the seven seconds it took the *Thunder Child* to right herself in the angry water.

"Woohoo! Ain't she somethin'?" Jim whooped as Doc regained his composure.

"Don't do that again!" Doc shouted as he straightened in his captain's chair and caught sight of the enemy boat, capsized and sinking.

"Sure am glad it's not one of mine!" Jim grunted as he watched it bob upside down.

"Now we've got to get 'em aboard somehow," Doc said. "Radio the Coast Guard, Jim."

"Do you make a habit of saving folks who try to kill you?" Jim asked, sarcastically.

"More often than you'd guess," Doc replied. "It's less paperwork if I don't kill them."

"You got a point there," Jim conceded. "Use that grab pole I yanked you aboard with."

"It'll have to do," Doc said and lifted it out of its cradle.

"Georgia's an 'Open Carry' state, Doc," Jim said. "Don't be afraid to use that .45 of yours if you have to. I'd love to get some more practice with this 44 Magnum of mine, too."

Doc fished the first stranger out of the sea and dragged him aboard. The scoundrel choked on the salt water in his lungs and gasped for air. But the minute he was sure Doc was focused on the two still in the water, his eyes raced about the cabin of the *Thunder Child* for anything he could use as a weapon.

"Eeeeasy, partner," Jim said to him slowly. "This Smith and Wesson only has a four-inch barrel. So the bullet might not go exactly where I aim it. If I aim it at your knee, I might shoot you in the dick. If I aim at your dick, I might shoot you in the head. It's the most powerful handgun in the world and wherever I hit you, it's going to make a mess. So sit still and maybe I won't have to shoot you at all."

With the first villain at his feet where he could keep an eye on him, Jim used every bit of his experience to carefully maneuver the *Thunder Child* in the pounding storm, while Doc got the other two aboard. They looked near death by the time he dragged them aboard, gasping for air and grateful to still be alive. But the first of the three had regained his strength and hatred.

"You pigs nearly drowned us!" he shouted over the roar of the storm.

"Lucky for you we're pigs with hearts," Jim replied sarcastically. "What are the three of you doin' out here anyway? And why'd you try to kill us? Were we getting too close? What were you afraid we'd see?"

"We were just enjoying ourselves," the stranger said. "I thought you meant us harm."

"Yeah right," Jim answered. "Tell it to the Coasties."

"I want your keys!" Doc yelled at the three of them as they struggled to their feet when the Coast Guard cutter pulled alongside the *Thunder Child*.

When they hesitated, Doc drew his 45 caliber and cocked it.

"Don't give me an excuse to use this," he growled at them. "You're almost safe and sound and headed for shore."

They each tossed their keys in Doc's direction, making them clatter on the cabin's floor.

"Your motel key cards too," Doc added, and they complied.

The storm was finally weakening as Doc marched the trio out of the cabin, across the long bow of the *Thunder Child* and made them jump to the cutter alongside.

"I'm Deputy U.S. Marshal John Holiday," Doc said and flashed his badge to the two Coasties who took the trio into custody. "Read those hombres their rights and hold 'em until you can deliver them to the Tybee Island Police."

"Aye-aye!" they said and put the men in cuffs as the cutter headed back to the station.

"That bucket we capsized belongs to my friend, Tony Seguna," Jim chuckled. "He should do business with better people. Wait 'til he hears he's got one less boat this season."

"We need to get back in and look through their car," Doc said. "Then we have to go through every inch of their motel room."

"What are we lookin' for?" Jim asked, happy to finally be included.

"We need to know what this bunch knows about the bomb," Doc said.

"Are you sure they know something we don't?" Jim challenged him.

"Not yet," Doc answered. "But they were sure busy at the coordinates earlier, and I spooked them just by looking at them. Whatever they're up to, you can be sure it's no good. And if it has anything to do with bringing that bomb up from the bottom, the President needs to know about it, because it this group doesn't do it, another bunch will unless we end this now."

6

INTO THE DEEP

J im and Doc found Louis, Q, and Noah waiting for them on the dock of the marina. They helped moor the *Thunder Child* in her berth after getting Jim to promise them a ride before they left town.

"Where'd you get such an incredible-looking machine, Dad?" Louis said with eyes wide.

"It's J.W.'s, and she sure came in handy," Jim answered. "You know that 'self-righting' claim J.W. always bragged about but never tried? It works like a charm!"

"You actually rolled this rocket out there in the storm?" Louis asked in disbelief.

"Not on purpose!" Jim laughed.

"That's a lie," Doc laughed back at him. "I'll never believe that one."

"We came up empty-handed," Q told Doc.

"Well, we caught three big ones out there," Doc said with a grin, and looked over his shoulder at the sea that was finally calming as the hanger doors slid closed. "They were awfully busy with something out at the coordinates. We had to chase them down and fish them out of the drink. They're in Coast Guard custody at the moment, and aren't talking."

"Do you think they know where the bomb is?" Noah asked.

"It appears that way," Doc said. "But they've had the coordinates for days. So I'm not sure why it would still be underwater...unless they discovered it will take more than they thought to bring it up. I'll let the President know the Coast Guard has three fellas in custody. I'll bet he has a task force on standby, probably at the Kings Bay Naval Base south of here, just waiting for his order to retrieve the bomb if we locate it.

"Louis, I need you and Noah to tear through the guys' rental car outside the Tybee Island Marina, while Q and I do the same to their motel room," Doc said.

"What are we looking for?" Louis asked.

"I don't have a clue," Doc said. "Look for anything that appears to be about the bomb, and anything that ties them to anyone else that might be helping them look for it. And keep your eyes peeled for others, too. There may still be some more of them running around the island. "

"What do you need me to do?" Jim asked hopefully.

"I'm truly grateful for your help, Jim," Doc said earnestly. "In fact, I believe you saved my life. But I can't have you any more involved than you already are. To tell you the truth, it would be a big help if you reopened for business and acted as if nothing's happened today. If anyone asks about the Coast Guard run or anything else that happened, just shrug your shoulders."

"Lord knows, I've had plenty of practice doin' that,"

Jim sighed in disappointment.

By the time Doc and Q arrived at the motel, Louis and Noah had already combed through the glove box and front seat of the strangers' rental car. Louis popped the trunk lid while Noah pulled the back seat bottom cushion completely out of the car to make sure nothing was hidden underneath it. The trunk was empty too. Louis peeled back the mat that covered the bottom of the trunk and found nothing but sheet metal. Noah tucked the rear seat cushion back in place as Louis closed the trunk. When their eyes met, Noah saw a spark of an idea in Louis' gaze and watched the Marine retrieve the rental paperwork from the glove box.

"Bingo!" Louis said excitedly as he opened the packet and pulled out three folded sheets of paper that were clearly not part of the contract.

"What have you got there?" Noah asked excitedly.

"Not quite sure," Louis said quietly as he tried to decipher the poor handwriting.

By then, Doc and Q had searched every drawer, closet, and cabinet in the motel room.

They were trying to think of a hiding place they must have missed when Noah called.

"What's up?" Doc said into his phone.

"I think we might have something here, Doc," Noah said tentatively.

"What da' ya' got?" Doc asked and punched the speaker phone icon. "I need some good news. We got goose eggs here."

"It's kinda hard to read, but I found some papers stuck in the packet the guys got from the rental company and one of the pages mentions a 'Forbidden Library,'" Noah said. "Have you ever heard of such a thing?"

"Just the day before yesterday," Doc said with surprise. "The President mentioned he'd heard about a group calling themselves 'Guardians of the Forbidden Library.' He said if the intelligence community is correct about the group, the world might be hanging in the balance. We had details in the can of 'worms' you destroyed yesterday, Q," Doc said. "The President ordered it done, in favor of this mission. So even he has no idea there's a connection. But what is it, exactly? Good work, you two. Lock the car and meet us at Louis' dad's marina."

As Doc and Q crossed the motel parking lot headed for their car, they passed a man carrying a helmet that looked a lot like the one Doc saw one of the men on the boat wearing.

"That's quite a helmet," Doc said to the man as he passed by. "What kind is it?"

"It's a new HYDROID Aquabreather," the man said proudly. "It totally eliminates the need for tanks. Do you dive?"

"A bit," Doc replied. "But I've never seen anything like that."

"It's only experimental," the man told him. "But I can tell you it works beautifully."

"Have you tried it out in the open sea?" Doc asked, hoping for more information.

"Yep, that's what it's meant for," the man said.

"But just recreational diving, right?" Doc asked. "I mean, you can't really exert yourself in that can you?"

"Sure can," the man corrected Doc. "I had it a hundred feet down for nearly an hour yesterday. It worked perfectly."

"How does it work?" Doc prodded him.

The man opened a compartment atop the rear of the helmet to reveal two canisters about the size of energy drinks.

"These cans contain a patented chemical compound that absorbs carbon dioxide and generates oxygen at the same time," the man explained. "A small monitor inside the helmet tells you your depth, what direction you're looking in, and how much time you have remaining before the canisters must be replaced."

"Wow!" Doc said sincerely. "So if I wore one of these I wouldn't need tanks or a rebreather?"

"Nope," the man said proudly. "You only need a wet suit, flippers, and a weight belt."

"Okay, but what's it cost?" Doc asked.

"Oh, you can't buy 'em yet," the man said. "We're testing them for the manufacturer. It's all still very low-key. I shouldn't even be talking about it. But it's just so amazing."

Q moved in close behind the man and stuck a snub-nosed .44 magnum revolver in his back just hard enough to make his point.

"Have you ever seen the damage a Fallout 4 can do?" he asked rhetorically. "It's even more amazing than the helmet of yours."

"Hand over the helmet and get in," Doc told the man and opened the rear door of his car.

"I've got friends here who will mess you guys up bad,"

the man told them both.

"Yeah, we know," Q snickered. "They're waiting for you at the Coast Guard station."

Q slipped into the back seat of the car with their newest prisoner and Doc called Noah back as he walked around the front of the car.

"Hey, Noah. Q and I will be there in just a bit," he said. "We've got another desperado to deliver to the Coasties first. In the meantime, ask Jim to grab me a wet suit and to refuel *Thunder Child*. You're going to get your ride after all."

"Hot dog!" Noah shouted. "See you soon, Doc!"

Doc called the Coast Guard station for its address, punched it into the car's GPS, and raced there. Commander Travis Broadmore met Doc and Q and their prisoner at the guard shack and took him into custody.

"Do we have all of them now, Marshal?" the Chief asked Q.

"Far as we know, Commander," Q replied. "Our information is that they're part of a little-known radical group that's been looking for the Tybee Bomb, which we think they may have located."

"You're kidding, right?" the Commander asked incredulously. "Don't believe it unless you see it with your own eyes. I've been stationed here for three years now and I can tell you we've never had even a little luck locating it. And we give it a try every few months."

"Well they may have had beginner's luck," Q said as Doc climbed back into the car and started it up. "Gotta go, Commander. If we confirm that they've found it, you'll be the next to know...after the President, that is."

When Doc and Q returned to the Sea Me Marina hanger, the big boathouse doors were open and the roar of *Thunder Child's* giant twin diesels was deafening as Jim revved them. Q stepped into the cabin first, with Doc close behind. Louis, Noah, and Jim were as excited as kids on Christmas morning.

"What kinda newfangled helmet you got there?" Jim said the moment he saw it in Doc's hands. "You plannin' on doin' some jet skiing?"

"Actually, it's a new diving helmet, Jim," Doc replied. "It's called an Aquabreather and I've been told it'll keep me comfortable under up to 150 feet of water for about an hour—no tanks required."

"I'll believe it when I see it," Jim said flatly.

"Yeah, me too," Doc replied. "And we'll see pretty soon. Do you have a wet suit and a good underwater light for me?"

"I do!" Jim said with a chuckle. "I was going to bring you a Speedo, but I thought better of it. The water's mighty cold 100 feet down."

"If I ever had Speedo days, they're far behind me, Jim," Doc laughed. "I'll suit up now. So let's get moving. The sooner we find out whether or not these guys found the bomb, the sooner Louis and the rest of us can get on with our original plans."

"Personally, I prefer this to my other plans," Jim said with a broad grin. "You know old seadogs die hard, Doc."

Doc knew all too well how right Jim was. Even as he donned the heavy wet suit in search of the Tybee Bomb, he knew that the moment he completed this mission, he'd turn his attention to the Guardians of the Forbidden

Library, and whatever they were up to that so concerned the President. And for once, Doc felt as though he had a head start on a mission. After all, he already had several members of the group behind bars.

"Pick a chair in the forward compartment and fasten your safety harnesses boys," Jim shouted over the roar of the engines as *Thunder Child* launched out the doors of the boathouse.

"I think these five-point harnesses are a bit overkill, don't you?" Q asked Doc, who was seated across from him.

"Let me know if you still think that in a few minutes," Doc replied with a wry smile.

As if on cue, Jim pushed the throttle fully open and the craft seemed to rise out of the water as it accelerated to a full 70 knots. The boat rocketed from one wave top to the next, moving more like a bucking bronco than a boat. The seats were mounted on a shock-absorbing system of springs and hydraulics to mitigate the continuous impacts as the boat bucked and jolted in every direction. Doc laughed out loud as he saw Q grit his teeth, lock his neck, and grip the sides of his seat.

"Geronimo!" Doc shouted as *Thunder Child* seemed to defy the laws of physics and gravity. "I've gotta get me one of these! How about you, Q?" he asked in jest.

"Not me!" Q shouted back. "I prefer to die on dry land!"

"Hang on, boys! I'm going to roll this crate one more time! Might be the last chance I get!" Jim yelled to his shipmates.

"If this doesn't work, send my pieces to Marsha!" Q

yelled to Doc, half in jest.

"You'll love this!" Doc shouted back. "This is what *Thunder Child* was built for!"

Jim suddenly put *Thunder Child* into a hard turn in the high waves and the ship rolled completely upside down...at 70 knots. The maneuver didn't result in any loss of speed and its GPS had it back on course when *Thunder Child* righted itself in seconds

"Hot damn, what a boat!" Jim yelled at the top of his lungs. "Wanna' do it again, boys?"

"No!" everyone shouted back, and Jim broke into a belly laugh

"Good thing no one's had supper yet!" he shouted. "We're approaching the target," he yelled, and eased back on the throttle. "We'll be there in about four and a half minutes!"

Doc began to prepare himself for the dive ahead. He took long, deep, deliberate breaths and began his usual pre-dive stretches. Only then did he begin thinking about the unknowns of using the Aquabreather, and the differences it might make in the dive.

Jim turned off *Thunder Child's* engines exactly four and a half minutes later, at coordinates where he and Doc had found the deadly trio that morning. Q, Noah, and Louis gathered around Doc as he slipped into flippers, fastened his weight belt, and attached his Schrade SC90 to it, then lifted the Aquabreather and light out of the cabinet he'd stowed them in.

"Wish I had the owner's manual for this," he chuckled as he carefully inserted his head.

Fortunately, the internal monitor flickered to life the

moment the helmet was in place.

Activate Breather flashed across a narrow display bar at the bottom of his visor and a small icon pointed out the switch's location on the helmet.

Doc turned the Aquabreather on and **Time Std./Time Set** flashed next with another icon. Doc figured it was a choice between the standard 60-minute dive and a shorter one. So he selected **Time Std.** Now the display flashed **SW, 0.0 ft.**, and **60.00 min.** and Doc understood he was facing southwest, hadn't yet begun his descent, and had 60 minutes to complete the dive. The helmet was surprisingly light and Doc began to feel comfortable in it as he made his way to the stern, and Noah, Louis, and Q each dropped an anchor over the sides to hold the boat steady in the waves.

"Wish me luck!" Doc said as he tumbled backwards into the water with both thumbs up.

"Good luck, Doc!" they all called out together.

They crowded around the boat's small radar screen and watched the small blip that tracked Doc's descent into the deep.

"God be with you, my good friend," Q said softly.

Chapter Seven – The Tybee Bomb

It was late afternoon and the water was growing dark, but Doc didn't intend to be under very long. He knew he didn't have much time to search for the bomb. So his hope was that if the men who were over the spot that morning found the bomb, they cleared some of the sediment away, making it easier to spot. He turned on his light at 40 feet and continued his descent.

At 80 feet, Doc was beginning to wish he had contact

with Jim in *Thunder Child.* The Aquabreather had a built-in headset. But Doc had no idea how to use it and there wasn't time to figure it out before the dive. So he continued the dive in radio silence...and suddenly got a spooky feeling he was being watched.

At 90 feet, Doc marveled at how well the Aquabreather was functioning. But it didn't warm him and he began to feel the cold. It brought his SEAL Team Shadow days to mind, when he dove in many different conditions. He had even swum a little more than a mile under the Arctic ice once. But that was nearly five years before this dive, when he was younger and glory and honor were foremost in his heart and mind.

Glory and honor still drove the former SEAL. But on this day, he had already begun to tire and the bottom was not yet in sight. Doc was older now and battle-worn. Cold and 100 feet below the surface, the days when he believed victory was inevitable seemed a lifetime ago. Now, victory wasn't so easily defined, and the foremost thoughts in his heart and mind were simply to complete the mission and live to see Connie again.

At precisely 101 feet, Doc reached the bottom of the Atlantic, 12 miles off the Georgia coast. Meanwhile, Connie stood on the big front porch of their Montana home, overlooking Flathead Lake, 3,000 feet above sea level, 90 miles south of the Canadian border. She grabbed the binoculars that hung on a nail beside the front porch swing and took a close look at the large, black SUV parked near the dock below. It had been parked there for more than three hours. So she knew another would replace it within the hour. There were always at least two people inside. Connie assumed they were FBI agents. But they could just as easily have been with the U.S. Marshals Service or Homeland Security.

Their presence told Connie all she needed to know about Doc's latest mission. At best, the President wasn't sure how dangerous the mission was, and he sent security just to play it safe. At worst, he knew precisely how dangerous the mission was and he wasn't playing at all. Connie chose to assume the former as she focused the binoculars. She was surprised at how young the female on the passenger side looked.

"See anything interesting?" Marsha asked over Connie's shoulder.

"Oh, you startled me!" Connie gasped and lowered the binoculars. "I didn't hear you walk up."

"I'm so sorry," Marsha said. "I didn't mean to scare you."

"It's alright," Connie replied. "I was just checking to see how many were in the truck. I was thinking about taking them a thermos of coffee and some of the bundt cake I took out of the oven a few minutes ago. Wanna help me?"

"Sure!" Marsha answered. "I've been dyin' for a look at the folks getting paid to sit and watch us."

"Me too!" Madeleine called out as she stepped onto the porch.

"Well, let's go meet 'em!" Connie said cheerfully.

The three of them packed up the cake and coffee, piled into the Escalade, and headed down to the dock for a few minutes of friendly conversation with their sentinels.

.   .   .

Beneath 100 feet of dark, cold water, Doc was running out of time, energy, and patience.

Where's the bomb?! he shouted in his head. *I've come this far, damn it, and those characters were at this spot for a reason! It's here somewhere! It has to be!*

Doc swam in an increasingly large radius until **24.00 min.** appeared on his monitor. At most, he had another eight minutes before he had to begin his slow ascent. If he was going to locate the bomb, it had to be soon.

"Where the hell are you?!" Doc shouted into his helmet in frustration.

That's when Doc got a visit from the largest leatherback sea turtle he'd ever seen. Adult leatherbacks typically grew to a maximum of 2,000 pounds and averaged six feet in diameter. This one was close to eight feet across and easily weighed more than a ton. Thinking his hunt for the bomb was a bust, Doc thought he'd console himself with a brief sea turtle encounter. So he set out after the behemoth, headed due east.

With just six minutes left to spend on the bottom, he followed along about ten feet behind the turtle. Then suddenly, with **18.45 min.** displayed in Doc's helmet, the turtle darted to the bottom and lay motionless. Doc floated about ten feet above and marveled at how beautifully the turtle blended into the rocky surface. Just as suddenly, a ten-foot great white shark appeared out of nowhere and swam a lazy circle around Doc and the turtle. Doc forced himself to remain calm and checked to make sure his knife was secure in the sheath, strapped around his thigh.

As his eyes followed the shark closely, Doc caught a glimpse of a coral-encrusted surface too narrow and flat to be natural. Rusted to a dull, drab reddish brown, the panel rose about six feet straight up from the bottom. Doc assumed an upright position and faced the shark straight on. He slowly swept his arms and legs in broad circles to make himself appear as big as possible to the shark and propel himself toward the rusted panel. When he reached it, he used his knife to scrape the barnacles and rust away—and was able to read the infamous insignia Mark 15. He'd found the bomb!

Doc undid the 150-foot coil of nylon rope attached to his weight belt and tied one end around a heavy, elongated piece of coral and began his slow ascent with the other end of the rope in hand. He hoped he was moving slow enough for the shark to lose interest. But the great white wasn't ready to let Doc swim away without closer inspection.

The struggle to remain calm was now almost too much for Doc to bear. As he ascended slowly to allow his lungs to adjust to the lessening water pressure, the shark swam in a slow circle, about 15 feet away. As Doc ascended, so did the shark. The razor-sharp, four-inch blade of Doc's Schrade SC90 was the only thing between him and the great white. And Doc was an expert at using it. He opened it and slid it securely up his left sleeve, where he could quickly retrieve it if he needed it.

With 50 feet to go, the great white rushed right at Doc and the reflexes of the former SEAL kicked in. In a flash, he took his knife in hand—but then suddenly thought better of the impulse to stab the shark's snout. Doc feared blood might attract more sharks. So instead, he brought the knife's blunt handle down hard on the shark's snout. It worked, for a few minutes. But 30 feet from the surface the great white attacked again and nearly trapped Doc's left arm in its jaws. Though Doc moved fast enough to avoid being bitten, the shark got a length of the nylon rope between its powerful jaws, and its seven rows of razor-sharp teeth easily severed the line like it was an overcooked egg noodle.

With just **11.05 min.** displayed in Doc's helmet, he held a loose end of rope in each hand as the savage shark retreated about 10 feet, then attacked Doc for a third time. This time, Doc drew his legs up into his chest and kicked them out with a force that struck the creature's snout so hard it turned on a dime and swam away for good.

Noah, Louis, Q, and Jim were all now huddled at the stern, hoping to catch sight of Doc rising toward them.

"He's got ten minutes left, at best. Where the hell is he?" Jim grunted in exasperation.

"He's a SEAL, Jim," Q reminded him. "He knows what he's doing."

"He's an *old* SEAL," Jim replied. "Doesn't he know his limits?"

"I'm not sure he has limits," Q said with admiration. "If he does, I haven't seen 'em."

Doc was so cold and drained of energy by that time; his hands trembled as he knotted the two pieces of the rope together and headed to the surface.

"There he is!" Noah shouted excitedly, and pointed about 50 feet away, off the port bow.

Jim leapt to the controls and eased *Thunder Child* within a few feet of Doc. Louis quickly took the rope from Doc, tied a small marker buoy equipped with a beacon to it, and tossed it back into the surf. It took all four men to lift Doc out of the water and pull him aboard.

"We found it!" Doc gasped as Jim carefully removed the helmet from his head.

The story of the turtle and the shark would have to wait. Doc needed all his strength to call and tell the President they'd found the bomb, and four Guardians...whatever *they* were.

"Great work, Doc!" the President said excitedly. "I've got a sub and a salvage team on standby alert at the Kings Bay Naval Base. They'll be underway within the hour."

"But we've got what might be an even bigger problem, Mr. President."

"Well, let's discuss it on a secure frequency," the President said. "Get to the Coast Guard station as fast as you can and call me back."

"I can be there in minutes, Mr. President," Doc said. "Talk to you then. Get me there pronto, Jim!"

"Aye-aye, Captain! Strap-in again, fellas!" he shouted as he slid behind the controls and *Thunder Child's* huge twin diesels roared to life again. "We're going to see EXACTLY how fast this tub can go!"

Doc timed the trip. Coasties moored *Thunder Child* at the dock precisely eleven minutes later.

"Woooo hoooo! I gotta get me one of these!" Jim shouted as he went ashore.

Doc was taken to the nearest secure satellite phone. Jim paced the dock and eyeballed every inch of *Thunder Child's* exterior while Louis, Noah, and Q talked about Georgia Bulldogs football with the Coasties who stood watch over the craft, as ordered by the President.

"Doc, did you know those criminals you captured down there this afternoon have been boasting to the Coast Guard that they intend to hold the whole nation hostage once they have the bomb?" the President asked.

"Well, we've got the bomb now. And to tell you the truth, Mr. President, we looked for it," Doc said as diplomatically as he could. "But we figured as much because of what I wanted to talk with you about."

"Go ahead Doc," the President said, "fill me in."

"All four of the clowns we arrested are connected with the group you mentioned to Connie and me in Washington."

"Yeah, and to tell *you* the truth, we're only about five minutes ahead of you," the President admitted. "I just had the photos of their wrist tattoos dropped on my desk. They're all members of the Guardians of the Forbidden Library, same as Yasin. We know it's an international group, and they apparently have a lot more going on than the hunt for the bomb. We suspect they're involved in the murders of at least a half-dozen writers here and elsewhere in the world."

"Mr. President, Yasin found Connie and me in rural Montana!" Doc said with alarm. "That bunch has to have a mole in the FBI...or the White House! My team and I have to get back to Montana now, Mr. President," Doc said.

"I understand, Doc," the President replied. "But I believe I have a better solution. I've already got birds in the air to get your wives to safety. Do you have a safe place even I don't know about?"

"It just so happens I do, Mr President," Doc said, and began to relax.

"Great. So here's my plan," President Preston said. "Soon after we hang up a Chinook chopper will be on its way to pick them up at your home. It's the fastest in the world, Doc. Two hours later they'll be at Spokane International Airport, where my personal 757 will be waiting to take them wherever you like. You can meet them at the Coast Guard Air Station in Savannah. I'll have Homeland Security there to escort you wherever you wish. Even they won't know where until they hear it from you. Fair enough?"

"More than fair, Mr. President," Doc said, finally breathing normally again. "Thank you."

"Thank *you*, Doc," the President said. "Give my thanks to your team as well, and tell Connie that Melanie and I look forward to seeing you both again soon. And Doc—thanks again for another excellent job. Our country owes you a debt of gratitude. If you need anything, you know how to reach me, and assuming you'll not go far, use this secure line. Be well, my friend!"

"It was our honor to be of service, Mr. President," Doc said, and ended the call.

The team looked at Doc with anticipation as he walked their way.

"Wherever you're going next, don't ask me to go with

you, Doc." Jim smiled and said, "I promised Anne a movie after dinner tonight."

"Actually, I was going to ask you if you can put us and our wives up for a few nights," Doc said almost apologetically.

"Of course we can," Jim assured him with a grin. "But we've got a wedding to attend this weekend. In fact, I think you may have met the bride and groom."

"Well, we probably should get back to the house so your wife can get her packing finished, because the three of you are going to Spokane in style. But you must go this evening. I'm sorry for such short notice, Jim. I will brief Louis on the reasons why, and he can fill you and Anne in. I can assure you that it's for everyone's safety and that the President of the United States will know about and appreciate the sacrifices this mission has required of your family."

"I understand, Doc," Jim assured him. "We're a God-fearing, flag-loving country, and we'll do what's required."

"I am certain of that, Jim," Doc said. "Please tell Anne that she's welcome to shop in Spokane for anything she's unable to pack this evening...courtesy of the President."

"*That'll make her smile!*" Jim chuckled.

"Excuse me for a moment," Doc said to Jim. "I've got to call Connie to tell her about the change of plans. Wish me luck."

Doc called, but Connie had left her phone on the dining room table when she and Marsha and Madelaine headed across the front lawn and down to the dock to deliver the coffee and cake to the agents standing watch over them.

7

GUARDIANS AT THE GATES

Connie, Madeleine, and Marsha gathered on the passenger side of the Suburban and introduced themselves to the agents who were surprised by their thoughtfulness.

"We can't thank you enough, ladies, really," the female agent said. "The coffee's perfect and I'll bet this bundt cake is too. I'm Agent Brewer and my partner is Agent Parker."

Before anything else could be said, another black Suburban approached them.

"Looks like you ladies brought this treat down to us just in time," Agent Brewer said.

"They're a half hour early," Agent Parker noted, squinting into the rearview mirror. "That's unusual. Ladies, you would do me a great favor if you would quickly climb into the backseat without questions."

The wives climbed aboard and Agent Parker switched the big SUV into 4-wheel drive mode and swiftly drove it up the steep incline, directly to Connie's front porch.

"What are you doing?!" Connie exclaimed as the Suburban literally cut deep tracks in the soft, grassy slope she loved to look out over from her porch.

"Our relief would never show up this early," Agent Parker told her. "Stay low and run into the house, ladies. We'll be right behind you."

The wives ducked and ran up the front steps and into the house. Both agents exited on the passenger side and were right behind them. But shots rang out from the second SUV and one tore into Agent Brewer's right leg. Agent Parker helped her up to the front porch and into the house while Connie quickly pulled down the bolt-action Seekins Precision Havak hunting rifle from its cradle above the living room fireplace. Like Doc had taught her, she grabbed a handful of 6.5 mm cartridges from the fishbowl on the mantle, ran to the open front window, knelt on the floor, and rested the rifle stock on the windowsill. She fired off two quick rounds at the second SUV. The first put a huge hole in its windshield. The second pierced its grill and lodged in the radiator. Her hope was that the shooters would have enough sense to turn around and speed away while they still could.

Instead, they pulled behind the other Suburban, piled out the far side of theirs and into the one in front of it, which was still running. The driver put the Suburban in gear while his partners were climbed into it and the savage gang sped down the long, winding driveway toward the dock and the road that would take them back to US-93.

"Not on my watch!" Agent Parker grunted as he

bolted out the door, off the porch, and into the shot-up SUV.

He jammed the steaming Suburban into gear, stomped on the gas pedal, and raced straight across the lawn in a wild bid to cut the other SUV off at the dock.

"You bastards can't get away with shooting a Federal officer!" he said through gritted teeth as he bounced and braced himself behind the wheel and the SUV rocketed across a rough, rocky section of landscaping between the house and the dock.

The shot-up Suburban reached 70 miles per hour by the time it reached the dock. Trying to out-maneuver the crazed agent, the driver of the other SUV veered left, toward the lake.

"Big mistake, you sorry sack of..." Agent Parker screamed as he stomped even harder on the accelerator, broadsided the other SUV, and pushed it off the dock, into twenty feet of water.

Connie, Marsha, and Madeleine ran down to the dock and helped Agent Parker get out of the smashed-up SUV. His face was bruised and slightly burned from the airbags, but his legs were steady as he stepped onto the dock and drew his 10 mm Colt Delta Elite Rail pistol.

"I hope all you maggots can swim, because I won't get wet to save you," he growled as the four dazed Guardians bobbed in the water. "Failure to follow my instruction will result in your being shot in sensitive, fleshy parts of your bodies. Now I want everyone to swim to the dock and come out of the water all at the same time."

They complied and were on the dock with their hands up when the relief agents arrived.

"Looks like we missed a little bit of action," the agent who was driving said. "Sorry we missed it. Is everything under control?"

"It's under control alright," Agent Parker said. "But my Suburban's underwater. Give me your keys and escort these ladies back up to the house. I'll need one of you three slackers to ride along with me and keep an eye on this bunch while I deliver them to headquarters."

Agent Parker had to raise his voice for the last part of his directions because a CH-47F Chinook was approaching fast.

What is this all about? he thought to himself as he wheeled around and saw the big chopper descending to the ground, just off the dock.

While the rotors still thundered and everyone else was crouched against the whirlwind it created, he ran to the pilot's side of the copter.

"I'm Agent Charles Parker of Homeland Security!" he shouted over the noise of the rotors. "My partner, Agent Kelly Brewer, has got a nasty leg wound and needs to get to the nearest hospital immediately!"

The pilot gave him a thumbs-up and navigated the copter closer to the front porch of the house. Connie, Madeleine, and Marsha were already inside with Agent Brewer. The two relief agents who entered with them tied a tourniquet around her wounded leg, carried her down the front steps, and loaded her into the copter.

"I'll be back for the wives in about 30 minutes," the pilot shouted to the agents, and ascended at breakneck speed.

"Did he say he was coming back for us?" Connie asked one of the agents.

"He did, ma'am," the agent replied.

"What on earth for?" Connie asked no one in particular, and the agent shrugged.

Agent Parker then rolled up in the one good Suburban with a relief agent in the passenger seat and four handcuffed Guardians in the back.

"I just got a call from headquarters telling me to have the three of you ready to leave for Georgia pronto!" he told them.

"Georgia?" Marsha, Madeleine, and Connie said almost in unison.

"Why?!" Connie demanded. "Has something happened to our husbands?"

"They're fine, Mrs. Holiday," Agent Parker assured her. "The President of the United States has instructed headquarters to evacuate the three of you immediately and reunite you with your husbands. You must be ready when the chopper returns. It will take you to a private hangar at Spokane International, where you will board the President's personal plane and be flown to a location known only to your husband and the pilot. It's for the safety of all concerned, Mrs. Holiday. It was a pleasure meeting the three of you. I have to go. Godspeed!"

"Thank you for being here for us, Agent Parker," Connie said.

"Likewise!" he replied and drove away.

"Ladies, we have some fast packing to do!" Connie said as she led the other wives into the house.

Almost exactly thirty minutes later, the three of them

stepped back onto the porch with two bags each as the chopper descended.

"I'm leaving the house unlocked," she told the two agents at the bottom of the front steps. "And I'm taking the key because I expect someone to be here guarding it around the clock."

"Understood," one of the agents replied. "Homeland Security will take good care of it."

"Have a safe trip!" the other agent added.

"There's fresh, hot coffee on the stove and homemade bundt cake on the counter," Connie told the agents as they secured the side door of the chopper before it lifted off the lawn. "Thank you both for your service!" she shouted as the chopper ascended.

Just about that time, on the north end of Tybee Island, two miles from the Sea Me Marina, an officer found Pulitzer Prize-winning novelist Foster Cabot dead in his 2018 Rolls-Royce Phantom inside his six-car garage. He'd been dead for at least twenty-four hours, thanks to a carefully rigged shop-vacuum hose that ran from the exhaust pipe to the partially opened driver's-side rear window. It appeared that the late author of highly successful and very prurient mysteries had taken an entire bottle of prescription sleeping pills before he nodded off inside the expensive suicide machine.

Less than an hour later, on her country estate in the north of France, the renowned French figurative, erotic artist Manette Boucher-Fabron was discovered by her lover in very similar circumstances. But her car was a much less expensive, but just as deadly, 2016 Jaguar F-

Pace and was still running with a little more than a half a tank of gas remaining.

That's the way the media reported the twin tragedies. What they didn't report was that the last page of Cabot's latest book was displayed on his laptop computer in his study, and a jpeg file of Boucher-Fabron's latest painting on exhibit in Paris was displayed on the screen of her iMac in her studio…and neither the caps to their prescription bottles nor the key fobs for their cars were found by investigators.

Doc, Connie, Q, Marsha, Noah, and Madeleine saw the TV news report the next evening while they were trying to lower their stress levels with wine, cheese, and small talk in the den of the Danforths' family room.

"Sometimes I think the whole world is going mad," Madeleine sighed and leaned deeper into Noah's side on the comfortable loveseat they shared. "I don't understand how people who achieve so much and have so much to live for can be so unhappy that they take their own lives."

"It is troubling, isn't it?" Marsha agreed. "It's sad but true that you never really know all that's going on in the lives of others, no matter how close to them you may think you are."

"Well for the record, I'm on top of the world even though my dream house is empty and being guarded around the clock so bad guys don't disturb it," Doc said. "I'm safe, sound, and comfortable here, with the love of my life and the closest friends I have in the entire world."

"And Jenny and Louis and their families and friends are no doubt excitedly getting ready for their wedding in Spokane the day after tomorrow," Connie added. "It was wonderfully generous of the Danforths to give us the run of their home while they're away."

Marsha pulled Q's arm more tightly around her shoulders and looked out the huge picture window to the deck and the ocean beyond.

"It's so peaceful here," she sighed. "I feel as though we're a million miles away from the craziness of the world."

Noah, Q, and Doc silently shared a glance and took comfort in knowing they'd successfully completed another mission. They'd kept the Tybee Bomb out of the hands of the Guardians. Though it still wasn't clear what the Guardians planned to do with the bomb, Doc and company had unquestionably struck a blow for peace and safety in the world. So, at that moment at least, despite the television news, all was right in this small corner of the world...or so it seemed.

The next morning, across town, Thomas and Raymon Byrnes walked into the Tybee Island Police Department, introduced themselves, and asked to speak with the Chief of Police.

"What's this about?" the officer at the front desk asked.

"Nothing much, really," Tom said. "We just happened to be in town on another matter and hoped to get a look at the evidence in the Cabot case."

"Good afternoon, gentlemen. I'm Chief Russell Trapp. How can I help you?" he asked as he stepped in behind the counter.

"It's good to meet you, Chief Trapp!" Tom replied and flashed his FBI credentials. "I'm Tom Byrnes and this is my brother, Ray. He's a Maricopa County Deputy Sheriff in Arizona."

"You've both come a long way," the burly chief said. "Step inside and have a seat in my office. I'm right behind you."

The chief got comfortable in his high-back chair and got down to business.

"If all you wanted was to talk to me, you could have called," he said flatly. "This isn't a routine visit, because the Bureau's local office would have called with a heads up before sending someone over. But I can tell you that although the Cabot case is not yet formally closed it is, for all intents and purposes, open and shut. So what *exactly* is it you hope to learn about it?"

You're right, Chief," Tom told him. "This isn't a routine visit. In fact, it's not even official because we're just acting on a weak hunch. We don't want to make a federal case out of this—no pun intended. But we'd appreciate it if you'd be kind enough to just let us look at the evidence for a few minutes. We don't even need to handle it. If you could just show us the coroner's photos and the bagged evidence for a few minutes, we'll be on our way."

"Any time the FBI comes sniffin' around, it's a federal case," the chief said with a dead-serious look on his face. "You two aren't leavin' until I get some answers. So both of you might as well get comfortable and be straight with me, or it's going to be a very long day for all of us."

"We'll gladly answer all your questions, Chief...if you'll show us the evidence," Tom said and hoped for the best.

"Follow me," the chief said as he jumped up from his chair and headed out of the office in the direction of the evidence room.

He paused outside the door and laid the ground rules.

"I won't have you two muckin' up a simple case and makin' a lot of needless work for my department," he told them. "So put your hands in your pockets and keep them there. If you need a closer look at something, just say so and we'll make it happen. Okay?"

"Okay!" Tom and Ray said in unison.

The chief began by filling two tabletops with two dozen 8x10 photos of the top of Cabot's writing desk in his den, as well as the inside of his garage and vehicle.

"Well, you're team is certainly thorough," Ray commented. "Is this all of them?"

"It is," the chief said. "What exactly, were you hopin' ta see?"

"It's not what we were hoping to see, Chief," Tom told him. "It's more a question of whether there's something we *don't* see."

"Something in particular?" the chief pressed for specifics.

Tom and Ray looked at one another and Ray shrugged.

"We're wondering if there's a photo that includes the cap of Cabot's prescription bottle.

"Nope!" the chief replied to the question he had hoped they wouldn't ask. "We couldn't find it. That still bothers us...but not enough to be suspicious. I'll bet you're lookin' for his key fob too. We can't find that either.

We haven't released this information yet, but we impounded his vehicle so that our motor vehicle department can pull the front seat out."

"You won't find the missing items," Tom stated confidently.

"How do you know that?" the chief asked with eyes wide.

"We're not at liberty to share that information just yet," Tom said quietly.

"Now look, you two!" the chief erupted. "Either you start sharin' what ya know or I'll lock your asses up until ya do...or until your bosses make me turn ya loose. And I'm willin' ta bet they don't even know you're down here pokin' around!"

Suddenly there came a swift, sharp knock on the door, and a duty officer poked his head into the evidence room.

"Excuse me Chief," the officer said hurriedly, then cast a wary glance at the two visitors in the room.

"It's okay, Joe," the chief nodded. "They're friendlies."

"The Coast Guard just delivered the four suspects rounded up on the water yesterday," Joe said. "I thought you might want to check 'em out while we process them and the few belongings they have."

"You bet I do," the chief replied, and stepped toward the door, then turned and told the brothers, "Stay right here. I'm not done with you two yet."

Alone again, the brothers processed what little they'd learned about the Cabot case so far and talked using sign language, knowing they were likely being recorded.

"They haven't connected the Cabot murder with any

of the others yet," Ray signed. "They still suspect it's only an isolated, local murder."

"I'm not sure the time is right to share the international angle," Tom signed back.

"We can't keep this under wraps much longer," Ray signed. "You know the Bureau's already got some of the pieces. If you sit on this too much longer, the Bureau's going to catch up on the clues, assign others to the case, and we'll be on the outside looking in."

"Yeah, I know you're right," Tom signed back, just before the chief returned.

"Fellas, you better follow me," he said to them energetically.

"What's up?" Tom asked as he and his brother hustled to keep up with the chief.

"I have a surprise for you," the chief said as he opened the door to a small office with three large manila envelopes lying on a desk. "Step right up, gentlemen, and behold."

The chief picked up the first envelope and withdrew the four suspects' mugshots.

"Recognize any of 'em?" he asked the brothers.

"Nope!" they both said without hesitation.

"Now, let me know if you recognize anything in this second envelope," the chief said as he withdrew three Ziplock bags one at a time and laid them side by side on the desk.

The chief had a flair for the dramatic. So when he withdrew a fourth bag he held it in front of them. Inside it was a wallet, a medicine bottle cap...and a Rolls Royce key fob.

"Damn!" Tom said loudly when he saw it.

"Bingo!" Ray shouted and banged a fist on the desk.

"There's one more thing," the chief said. "Or actually, *four more things*?"

Out of the third envelope, he pulled four 8x10 photos of identical "Guardian" tattoos.

"Now," the chief said emphatically, "I need you to explain these. And neither of you is going anywhere until you do."

"I guess the time is right after all," Tom said to his grinning brother.

8

NOTHING JUST HAPPENS

The weather on Skidaway Island was perfect that morning. After a fabulous breakfast of hearty oatmeal, cream, fresh fruit, walnut pieces, and bagels from the best bakery on the island, Doc, Noah, and Q led their wives up to the broad, second-floor deck that stretched across the entire rear of the house, facing the ocean. Eight Adirondack chairs, painted in an array of island colors, were arranged invitingly near the railing, facing out toward Tybee Island to the northeast and the sea beyond. They each chose a comfortable chair and basked in the glorious morning sunshine, while a soft, salt air breeze made them even more comfortable as it blew in from the ocean that lapped at the edge of the Danforths' property.

With the sunshine and breeze in their faces, Noah, Q, and Doc each had several thoughts and memories about how they had enjoyed sitting together the week before on the deck behind Doc and Connie's home on Flathead Lake.

"Let's hope we don't get interrupted like the last time we sat on a deck," Q said.

Before responding, Doc replayed that day in his mind, how it began with relaxed conversation and Q's gift of the sword cane, and how it ended with his fight with Abdul Yasin, who was now in federal custody.

"Yeah," Noah agreed with Q. "That was really weird the way Yasin suddenly appeared out of nowhere.

"Actually, it wasn't all that weird," Doc told him. "Q spotted him in town the day before, but couldn't recall his name or where he'd seen his face until he identified him using government data bases."

"Yeah," Q said. "It *was weird* being sure I'd seen him before, but didn't know where."

"I think the weirdest thing about it was that Homeland Security found documents in Yasin's rental car tying him to that international radical group, the Guardians of the Forbidden Library. What in the world is that all about? And to top it all off, we found four more members down here trying to retrieve the Tybee Bomb."

"So you just gotta know that we've bumped into the tip of the iceberg," Q said.

"And we bumped into it twice in the same week and on opposite sides of the country," Noah added. "How weird is that? And you just have to wonder where else in the world Guardians are sneaking around…and why?"

"You boys aren't talking shop again, are you?" Madeleine leaned in and teased the husbands. "I thought your mission was accomplished?"

"Loose ends, my dear," Noah replied softly. "We're just discussing loose ends."

"Well, as I always tell Quinton," Marsha chimed in, "the loose ends will be addressed by the folks who get paid to do that."

"And as I always remind you, darling, loose ends can sometimes cost people their lives," Q replied. "Besides, it's a good mental exercise, which, at my age, I can never get too much of."

"Hey, everybody!" Connie finally interjected. "Let's just try to relax and enjoy being together in this beautiful place while we can. Before you know it, the world will find us again and demand our attention like it always does."

"You're absolutely right, Beauty," Doc said. "Jim and Anne will be back soon, and soon after that, we'll all be back home too. So let's make the most of the little time we have here and enjoy each other's company, while the rest of the world has no idea where we're at."

As Doc finished his sentence, they all heard the doorbell ring inside.

"Don't answer that," Connie said quickly. "No one's supposed to know we're here."

Doc couldn't help himself. He looked out a front window and saw the Tybee Island Police Chief's clearly marked Chevy Equinox parked outside. So Doc went to the door and opened it, which reopened his latest can of worms.

"How do you do?" the chief asked when Doc opened the door. "I'm Tybee Police Chief Russell Trapp and this is FBI Special Agent-in-Charge Thomas Byrnes and his brother Raymon, a deputy sheriff from the Phoenix area. They're down here temporarily to assist my department with the investigation of an open case. Is Mr. Danforth home?"

"No, um, I'm afraid he's in Spokane, Washington for his son's wedding," Doc replied. "My friends and I are housesitting while he and Mrs. Danforth are gone. My name is John Holiday. Can I help you with something?"

Connie overheard just that brief conversation and prayed under her breath that Doc wasn't about to be drawn into another dangerous mission. He wasn't. It was the same one.

"Well, Mr. Holiday," the chief began, "I understand that you and your associates and Mr. Danforth captured the four suspects the Coast Guard just transferred to my jail today. And to be honest, I thought the three of you had left town already. But since I have you here, I'd like to ask you a few questions about my newest prisoners," the chief said.

"We'll do our best, Chief," Doc said. "But I gotta tell you that you may know more about them than we do."

Doc moved to the foot of the stairs in the foyer and yelled, "Hey Q, Noah, can you come downstairs for a few minutes please?"

Moments later the men all sat in the dining room and the chief got right to the point.

"Gentlemen, what little I know about the three of you came from the Coast Guard, who told me only that you are loosely connected to law enforcement, and you came here at the request of Prestonhimself. That counts for somethin'. But you are still in my jurisdiction and I must demand that what we discuss here stays here. Understood?"

"Understood," the trio replied. "But *you* must understand that we are duty-bound to report all new information we gather to President Preston. That's the obligation we accepted when we agreed to find out all we could about what that bunch was up to regarding the bomb."

"But we're not here to talk about the bomb," the chief said as he set a manila envelope on the table.

"You're not?" Q blurted out in surprise.

"No, not directly," the chief said. "But we've stumbled onto an apparent connection between their interest in the bomb and the suspected murder of a local celebrity."

"Foster Cabot?" Doc guessed. "I thought he committed suicide."

"So did we," the chief replied. "At least we couldn't prove otherwise...until the four of you apprehended emptied their pockets."

"What did you find?" Q asked.

"The only two items that were missing from the scene when my patrolman found Foster Cabot deader than a doornail in his Rolls," the chief said. "The cap to the sleeping pills he took and the key fob to the car."

"They were missing?" Doc asked in surprise.

"Very!" the chief shot back. "We knew it was inconsistent with suicide, but we had no leads. So we withheld those details from the media and announced Cabot's death as a *suspected suicide*, hoping something more might turn up. Then the Coasties delivered your suspects to us, along with some very interesting pieces of evidence."

"Why do I get the feeling you're about to tell us you

found the missing bottle cap and key fob?" Q asked sardonically.

"Well, you're right," the chief told him. "But we also found something far more interesting. And that's where you come in."

"What would that be?" Doc asked.

The chief picked up the envelope from the table, took out the four 8x10s of the suspects' matching tattoos, and laid them side by side.

"Have you fellas ever seen tattoos like these before?" he asked, assuming they had.

"No," Doc said and squinted. "But we've heard an awful lot about 'Guardians' lately. Are you telling us our four suspects have matching 'Guardian' tattoos?"

"That's exactly what we're telling you," Thomas interjected. "Are you trying to tell us you didn't know that?"

"*That's exactly right*," Doc said forcefully. "So why would a gang of thugs who were supposed to be retrieving a nuclear bomb from the bottom of the ocean want to murder a local writer? It makes no sense."

"You don't know the half of it," Raymon said in frustration.

"What's that supposed to mean? And why in the hell are you and your brother here?" Q jumped in and asked.

"Guardians are implicated in other murders, Mr. Holiday," Thomas finally said. "We know of at least two: One in central Arizona, the other in northern France...all within the past week. We're beginning to think there may be others, committed earlier, that we haven't learned of yet. It appears the Guardians have it in for writers and artists."

"But why?" Noah said, unable to hold it in any longer. "Is there at least a pattern?"

"We have no idea right now," the chief admitted. "We wanted to speak with you fellas before formally calling in the FBI. But I must tell you, Thomas and his brother flew down here on their own dime precisely because the Bureau hasn't been willing to shine a light on this as far as anyone can tell. So for all we know, the six of us right here at this table know more about this matter than anyone else in the world."

"So what you're saying," Doc related, as he began to put it all together out loud, "is that it appears we have stumbled upon an international group of deadly radical terrorists who are not only randomly murdering creative types here and abroad, but were also down here trying to get their hands on a weapon of mass destruction?!"

"Yeah," the chief said, and sat back in his chair.

"Now that's a scary proposition!" Q uttered, and stared out a dining room window.

"Yeah," the chief said again. "This was such a peaceful town for so long. Tom and Ray, I don't know where this leaves you, but I've got to get the Bureau involved at this point."

"We understand, Chief," Thomas said. "Ray and I came down here hoping to ultimately get this on the right track. It appears we've accomplished that better than we ever imagined. Hopefully our superiors will agree with us. Hell, they might even agree to keep us on the investigation...if they let us keep our jobs."

"And I've got to call the President and fill him in from our end," Doc said, rising from the table. "I'd appreciate it if you fellas go with me to the Coast Guard station to be part of the call," he told Q and Noah.

"You bet!" Q answered for himself and Noah.

Doc was surprised to find Connie, Marsha, and Madeleine sitting outside the dining room.

"Well, if you didn't want us to listen you should have closed the door," Connie told him.

"Hello, Doc!" President Preston said energetically. "It's good to hear your voice. Have you and your group gotten some rest?"

"A bit Mr. President," Doc replied. "But I called to brief you on some recent developments."

"I thought you'd wrapped up your operation," the President said.

"So did I, Mr. President," Doc replied. "But some missions just don't want to come to an end, and I'm afraid this is shaping up to be one of them."

"How so?" the President asked, and leaned forward in his chair.

"Well, Mr. President, we thought we had simply beat the Guardians to the bomb," Doc said. "But Tybee Island Police Chief Russell Trapp just presented us with evidence that seems to implicate our suspects in the murder of another writer. This one's a local: Foster Cabot."

"Damn it!" the President spat into the phone. "We just learned last night that they whacked French painter Manette Boucher-Fabron. We can't keep up with them— let alone get ahead of them."

"I don't think we'll ever get ahead of them, Mr. President," Doc countered. "Of the millions of writers and painters worldwide, how could we ever know who might be next? Even worse, I'm willing to bet that it won't stop there. I believe we're going to see recording artists, sculptors, maybe even actors and directors targeted before long...if it hasn't happened already."

"Off the record, Doc—and I do mean *off the record*. The Bureau, CIA and INTERPOL are all looking into that as we speak," the President said softly. "We're advising all state, county, and local law enforcement of that possibility, but it's not for public consumption. We don't need the kind of hysteria this could cause...especially knowing as little as we do about it."

"But that makes potential targets sitting ducks!" Doc protested.

"So who do we tell? Who's the next target—and why? And if we tell them, what do they do in response?" the President asked rhetorically.

"Point made," Doc conceded. "It just seems so damned hopeless. It's like watching fish getting shot in a barrel."

"So tell me this, Doc," the President said. "Do you feel safe where you are?"

"Not really, Mr. President, considering how easily the police chief found us. But I don't know that we'd be safer anywhere else," Doc said. "Q? Noah? Would you feel the wives would be safer if we moved to a new location?"

"Not really," Q replied, and Noah signaled his agreement.

"Looks like we're staying put for the time being, Mr. President," Doc said.

"Alright then," the President said. "With your permission, I'll call the police chief and make sure he understands he's not supposed to discuss your location with anyone."

"Thanks, Mr. President," Doc said with a smile. "Am I authorized to tell folks the President of the United States just asked for my permission?"

"Don't get used to it, Doc. Be well, my friend," the President chuckled and ended the call.

"You also, Mr. President!" Doc responded.

While Doc and company headed back to Sugar Tree from the Coast Guard station, Connie prepared dinner. But Marsha and Madeleine drove into town to buy a copy of *Mine for Once,* Foster Cabot's latest and last best-seller. It had only been in stores two weeks. So they were surprised to learn the bookstore had sold out of all 100 copies.

"When do you expect to have more?" she asked a clerk.

"Not sure," the clerk replied. "They're out of stock and on back order. So it could be a long wait. When people found out he was dead, they flocked in here for his last book."

"Let's try the library," Madeleine suggested.

But the library's three copies were all checked out.

"As a matter of fact," the girl at the desk told them, "they're all overdue too!"

During dinner, Marsha told everyone what she and Madeleine had discovered in town.

"I thought it would be interesting to read an author's last book," Marsha confessed, "if in fact it got him killed.

But it just so happens they have completely sold out at the bookstore and are all checked out of the library."

"Well like I always say, Marsha..." Doc started to say.

"*Nothing just happens!*" everyone else at the table recited together with a laugh.

"Since you all find my theory so comical, I'll give you a challenge," Doc said. "After dinner, while I shower, I challenge you to go online and try to purchase the final books of the two other authors we know have been murdered: *Into Us* by Madison Ainsley, and *Murder's Upside* by her father, Culver Ainsley. Let me know what you find. When you've finished, please leave the computer on because it should almost be time to Skype with Jenny and Louis to congratulate them at their wedding reception."

"That sounds like an interesting challenge," Marsha said with a broad smile.

"Oh, if only that were all there is to it!" Connie said sincerely, and rolled her eyes.

9

WHAT IS MURDER, IF NOT INSANE?

D oc took his time showering, shaving, and dressing in order to give Marsha as much time as possible to research the other two authors' book sales, and to discuss her results with the others. Doc had an off-the-wall theory about the writers' last books— and how the Guardians might be involved—but he wanted their input before sharing what he was thinking.

"So what did you find?" Doc asked Marsha when he rejoined the group.

"I discovered the most amazing thing!" Marsha proclaimed. "All the books are sold out! Culver Ainsley's book sold out the day his death was reported."

"A second printing is in the works," Madeleine added, "but the publisher gives no release date. And the industry rumor is that Madison's publisher is in negotiations with a wealthy fan and collector for the publishing rights, so her book may never be released."

"I can't begin to imagine how much money that would require," Connie thought out loud, "or why a collector would go to such extreme lengths to keep the manuscript private, no matter how big a fan he or she is."

John settled beside Connie in the comfortable loveseat she had kept warm for him, and quietly listened to the group's discussion.

"People with money are as capable of compulsive behavior as anyone else," Madeleine suggested. "In fact, the more money they have the more compulsive they can afford to be."

"The Kansas City Chiefs' new rookie quarterback, Patrick Mahomes, is reportedly worth more than $10 million, and he's collected more than 180 pairs of sneakers," Q said.

"Maybe," Noah interjected, "but an over-the-top sneaker collection is a long way from buying the rights to a popular author's last novel, just to ensure you have the only copy."

"What if owning the only copy isn't the point?" Doc asked as a challenge.

"If that's not the point, what is?" Q asked.

"What if the point is to ensure *no one else* ever reads the books?" Doc conjectured. "What if the collector considers the novels' contents forbidden? What if the 'Forbidden Library' is a private horde of books no one else will ever read, written by authors who will never write again—and paintings no one will ever see, painted by artists who will never paint again? And then there are all the forbidden audio and video recordings, and forbidden motion pictures that will eventually only be found in the 'Forbidden Library.'"

"*That would be insane!*" Noah countered.

"What is murder, if not insane?" Doc countered back.

"True," Q chimed in, "But no one could afford what that would cost—not to mention the cost of having the creators murdered."

"Don't be too sure," Doc cautioned. "Money can buy many things—and lots of money can buy very many things."

"But a plan like that would cost millions," Connie guessed, "and the money will eventually run out, especially at the speed this murder spree seems to be moving."

"Unless the plan also includes a means of extorting millions of dollars to keep the spree going," Doc theorized.

"Like recovering and threatening to unleash a long-lost hydrogen bomb?" Q asked.

"For instance..." Doc tossed back with a head tilt and shoulder shrug.

"Why do I get the feeling you're suggesting we still have work to do?" Noah asked.

"I was afraid that was where this conversation was headed," Connie said.

"Never fear, Beauty," Doc said soothingly. "We're only brainstorming."

"Experience has taught me your brainstorms often become missions," Connie observed.

"Oh wow, look at the time," Doc said in the hope of changing the subject. "We need to log in to Skype and congratulate the new bride and groom."

Everyone crowded around the computer while

PRESTON W. CHILD

Marsha logged in and connected with Jenny Charles—
who by then was the new Jenny Danforth.

"HELLO!" Jenny excitedly yelled to them all as she
and Louis sat happily in front of the laptop Jim Danforth
had set up on the bridal table.

"CONGRATULATIONS, YOU TWO!" Connie, Doc,
Noah, Madeleine, Q, and Marsha all yelled back with
huge smiles.

"We're all so happy for the two of you!" Connie said.
"May you be blessed with a long, happy, prosperous life
together!"

"Well, we're certainly off to a great start!" Jenny
replied. "We wish you all could be here, and we hope
you're enjoying some downtime back there in Georgia."

"Hey, we never asked where you're honeymooning,"
Doc noted. "Is there even time for that before you're
deployed?"

"No, not really," Jenny sad with a moping grin. "Louis
has to report to the security detail at the Bangor Trident
Base near Seattle Monday afternoon. And me? I'm not
making this up. I have to report Tuesday morning at the
Trident Training Facility at Kings Bay Naval Submarine
Base, back there in Georgia, less than two hours from
Skidaway Island!"

"Oh my goodness!" Connie sighed. "I'm sorry to hear
you'll be so far apart."

"Well, it's just for a little while," Louis said as
consolation.

"And I'll be able visit my in-laws on weekends!" Jenny
said, happily.

"You better!" Jim and Anne answered together, off screen.

"I hope my folks left you a refrigerator and freezer full of your favorite things!" Louis added. "Of course, Mom's not there to cook for you all, but I'm sure you're managing just fine. Doc and Q and Noah, thanks so much for the exciting time you included me in back there. I wouldn't have missed it for the world! Gotta go dance and thank everyone else now, before things start to wind down here. Thanks so very much again, everyone! Bye for now!"

"Hey, folks!" Jim Danforth called out as he stuck his face into view. "You're missing one hell of a party! But I know you are enjoying the peace and quiet of island life. Be good to one another! Anne and I will see you in a couple of days!"

"You bet we will!" Anne added, and jumped into view. "We'll bring you some funny videos of Jim's dance moves too! Bye for now!"

And then they were gone.

"Well that was a whirlwind visit!" Connie said.

"Sure was!" Madeleine said. "It's a good sign that they're enjoying a wonderful, exciting celebration. Especially after all the rough and tumble that happened here without warning, just days before the wedding they'd planned for months."

"You are definitely right about that," Marsha agreed as she shut the computer down. "Now *we* can get back to our nice, quiet evening."

Shortly after Marsha turned off the computer, Doc got a text message from Jim.

hey Doc the combo for my gun safe in the study is 23-13-43 in case you need it but i hope you don't i got some weapons in there you will find interesting sorry i didn't think of it before I left

That's odd, Doc thought at first, but then defaulted to his firm belief that everything happened for a reason, which left him wondering what the reason could possibly be.

"Anything interesting?" Q asked Doc, who was still staring at Jim's text.

"Maybe," Doc said thoughtfully. "Jim just texted me the combination to his gun safe. He says he's got some weapons we might find interesting."

"Well, what do ya say we go check 'em out?" Q replied, and headed for the study.

"Hey, guys! What's up?" Noah asked as he walked into the room.

"We're headed to Jim's gun safe in his study," Doc told him. "He just texted me the combination and said he thought we'd find some of the weapons interesting. Wanna join us?"

"Sounds interesting alright," Noah said and fell in step with them.

In a far corner of the study, Jim's gun safe was securely built into the wall behind his replica of the "Resolute" desk used by President Preston and JFK before him. The bulletproof, fireproof cabinet was seven feet tall, three feet wide, three feet deep, and constructed of hardened steel two inches thick. Its combination lock felt solid and spun with taught accuracy as Doc dialed in the numbers Jim texted to him. It opened with a series of mechanical clicks and its heavy double doors opened smoothly and silently. A light automatically illuminated the austere interior when Doc swung the doors open. The interior was comprised of a 5'8" bottom cavity that held an assortment of semi-automatic rifles and a half dozen shotguns, all neatly arranged by caliber. Above it were two shelves. One held an impressive collection of two dozen handguns. The other was filled with boxes and boxes of various bullets and shells for the weapons.

"Well, Jim's one collector I'm glad is on our side," Doc said with a chuckle.

"Talk about serious firepower!" Q said as he took a unique-looking shotgun from the safe.

Benelli M2 XRail was engraved on the barrel of the 42.5-inch-long shotgun. Below the 21-inch barrel was a bundle of four 20-inch-long cylindrical chambers that held a total of 24 shells. As each chamber emptied, the bundle would automatically rotate to the next loaded chamber. It was a beautifully engineered nine-pound, black carbon steel behemoth. Two more just like it stood solemnly on either side of the spot it occupied on the ebony rack. Detail-oriented as Doc was, he immediately noted the doors had an emergency safety release on the inside.

"My God, that gun looks like it could wreak serious havoc," Doc said in admiration.

"These spinning chambers must hold about two dozen shells!" Q marveled. "It looks far more efficient and balanced than a clip. Is there a manual in there for this baby?"

Noah spotted the manual in a slot inside one of the doors and opened it.

"It holds 24 shells, plus one in the chamber," he read aloud.

"Whoa-ho!" Q crowed. "This 25-round widow-maker will persuade anyone to back off!"

"I never want to be on the receiving end of it," Doc agreed. "I wonder why he has three.

"There's a handwritten note on the inside cover of the manual," Noah noted.

To Jim, as my gift to the most-generous,
kindhearted gun collector I know!
Your friend always, J.W.

"I guess ole J.W. figured three guns was a more appropriate gift than just one," Doc said.

"What is the affection you Americans have for guns?" Noah asked, only half in jest.

"A gun is like sex," Q quipped. "It's only important when you really, really need it."

"We should take this to the Coast Guard gun range tomorrow and try it out," Doc said.

"Roger that!" Q happily answered enthusiastically.

"Count me in!" Noah added

On the way to the gun range the next day, Doc, Noah, and Q stopped at a gun shop and bought 200 buckshot rounds and 25 half-inch-thick metal targets. Doc quietly wondered if they needed so many. After all, it was unlikely anyone in the group would be able to fire more than one full load of 25 rounds. But he planned to leave the leftover rounds for Jim as their thanks for the use of the gun. Noah, who'd never fired even a cap gun in his life, lifted the box of rounds from the counter and discovered how heavy the lead was. It was a hint of the weapon's power.

"I can hardly believe how much these weigh," Noah told Q and Doc.

"If that got your attention, you're in for a real treat when you experience the kick of the gun as you fire off 25 rounds," Q advised him. "It's definitely *not* a toy."

"I'm not sure this will be fun," Noah told them.

"First you will need to learn to respect it," Doc said. "The fun will come once you understand and appreciate what its power can do."

"If you say so," Noah replied with a healthy degree of cynicism.

10

BUILT AND WIRED FOR BATTLE

Doc checked the three of them in at the Coast Guard gun range and checked out three pairs of protective, sound-deadening ear muffs.

"Are these really necessary?" Noah asked.

"Oh yeah!" Q assured him. "This baby won't just talk. She'll roar."

"You make it sound alive," Noah told him.

"You'll think it is when you pull the trigger," Doc replied. "You want to go first?"

"Ah, no. I don't think so," Noah wisely answered. "I'll watch first."

"Well here goes then," Q said as he donned his earmuffs.

Doc and Noah donned theirs too, as the deputy marshal raised the shotgun, braced its stock tight against his shoulder, took aim, and squeezed the trigger expecting a rapid-fire series of twenty-five strong kicks as the rounds exploded out of the barrel. He wasn't disappointed.

"*HOLY COW!*" he exclaimed as he lowered the weapon away from his pounded shoulder.

Even from thirty feet away, the metal targets down-range looked like Swiss cheese.

"This is a beauty!" Q raved. "My shoulder already feels like a mule kicked it."

"And this is *fun* to you?" Noah asked, doubtfully.

"Oh yeahhhhh!" Q quickly drawled. "It's good to know this kind of firepower is handy."

"Well, I hope you don't expect to use it any time soon," Noah answered.

"Ya never know, Son," Q answered as he rubbed his sore shoulder. "Ya never know."

Doc set up new targets and ran back to the firing line while Q reloaded the XRail.

"Your turn, Noah!" he said enthusiastically, eager to see the rookie in action.

"I guess there's a first time for everything," Noah said softly, and raised the gun.

"Hold it tight to your shoulder where it feels the most comfortable," Q told him.

"This gun will never feel comfortable," Noah replied with certainty.

"Don't be too sure of that," Doc advised him. "If you ever need it to save your life or the lives of others, you'll be amazed at how much comfort it can provide."

"If you say so," Noah answered doubtfully.

"Fire when ready!" Q called out. "And hold the trigger steady until you're out of ammo!"

Noah braced himself as he'd seen Q do it, squeezed the trigger, and unleashed the fury.

"You did good!" Q yelled, surprised at the damage Noah had inflicted on the targets.

"Maybe, but a broadsword or a pole axe never made me this sore," Noah answered.

"Man, you are a HEMA devotee," Doc chuckled. "This gun will never allow your enemies to get close," Doc assured him. "No matter how many of them there are."

"How many enemies can one man have?" Noah asked sarcastically.

"In this world, there's no telling," Doc replied. "So it's good to be ready for anything."

"What's HEMA?" Q asked.

"Remember Noah's broadsword and that Templar Knight in Acre?" Doc smiled.

"Oh, yeah," Q laughed. "I'll take this XRail over brute force every time."

"Are we ready now?" Noah asked impatiently.

"Maybe...after I take my turn," Doc answered, and hoped they'd never find out.

When Doc raised he powerful gun to his shoulder, pulled it tight into a comfortable spot, and looked down the barrel, he felt an instant connection with the weapon.

"Oh yeah," he said softly as he rested his index finger on the trigger.

The former SEAL slowly exhaled, steadied himself with his feet apart, and took aim.

Q and Noah instantly remembered the warrior in Doc as he took control of the weapon and opened fire. On his first try, with an unfamiliar and powerful gun, Doc shredded the targets. Noah and Q watched in silence as Doc calmly reloaded and fired off twenty-five more rounds, then twenty-five more. In the calm of their peaceful days, they'd forgotten Doc was built and wired for battle.

"Well, I'm ready to go now," Doc said with a satisfied smile. "How about you guys?"

"I'm ready for some lunch," Q said with a hand on his belly.

"Now that I can handle," Noah agreed.

"After lunch, I'll give you a lesson in cleaning and oiling a weapon," Doc told Noah.

"I can hardly wait," Noah answered sarcastically.

"Take care of your weapons and they'll take care of you," Doc recited.

"Amen!" Q chimed in.

"You two are definitely Americans!" Noah said with a smile and a shake of his head.

"Live free or die!" Doc chuckled and raised a fist into the air.

"Remember the Alamo!" Q howled the first thing that came into his head.

Back at the house, Doc put the remaining shotgun shells in the safe and took out the gun cleaning supplies, and taught Noah how to properly clean and oil the shotgun. Then he locked it in the safe and sent Jim a text about their experience with the XRail.

THANKS good friend it was fun on the shooting range today

i put the leftover shells in the safe

Doc was surprised by Jim's quick response.

glad to hear you enjoyed it doc haven't fired it myself yet

i got another surprise for u in my other safe in the basement

if ur interested

Doc shot back his obvious answer.

always interested in surprises if they are good ones

Jim's answer was almost immediate.

the combo is 24-14-44 ur 45 caliber should fit just fine

another good time is RIGHT AROUND THE CORNER

Doc raised an eyebrow at the cryptic message. But he *had* said he liked surprises.

thanks again jim see you two when you get back

Doc headed to the basement alone. He didn't want to get Q excited and intent on making another trip to the gun range, which Doc wasn't particularly interested in doing again so soon with some *ordinary* gun. Doc hadn't seen the basement before, but he figured it would be easy enough to find a gun safe. However, Jim's nicely finished basement was huge. Doc walked through a large family room, equipped with a wet bar, a home theater, a large full bathroom with a jetted garden tub and a sauna, as well as two more bedrooms. But he didn't see a gun safe.

I couldn't have missed it, he thought, and retraced his steps. *What am I missing?* he thought some more. *I don't see it. But Jim clearly said the second safe was in the basement,* Doc argued with himself, and retraced his steps again, thinking he may have missed a room.

"Doc? Are you down there?" Madeleine called down to him from the top of the stairs.

"Yeah, Madeleine!" Doc shouted from across the basement.

"We're going out to the deck to relax again," she said. "Connie asked me to find you."

"Okay," Doc answered, then recalled their first meeting in Rome and how she used what she called "Doyle's Equation" to help him find the lost Templar treasure.

"Okay, but can you come down here for a minute, and bring Doyle with you?" he asked.

Madeleine laughed as she descended the carpeted stairs, appreciating the fact that Doc had just admitted at least a small respect for her approach to solving mysteries.

"What are you looking for?" she asked Doc in the middle of the large family room.

"Jim told me he has a gun safe down here, but I can't find it," Doc admitted.

"What's it look like?" she asked.

"Well, the one upstairs is seven feet tall, three feet wide, and three feet deep," Doc said.

"But what does *the one down here* look like?" she asked again.

"I guess I don't know," Doc finally admitted. "I just figured they were the same size."

"And you've checked *every* room?" Madeleine asked.

"Twice," Doc answered. "So what would Doyle do?"

"Wow!" Madeleine said in mock surprise. "You're actually calling on Doyle?"

"Well, it paid off the last time we used his equation," Doc conceded.

"Okay, here goes," she began. "You're sure you checked every room?"

"Yes!" Doc answered.

"And you're certain there is no safe?"

"Yes!" Doc said impatiently. "Well, no. But I'm sure I would have seen it regardless of its size if it were here."

"But Jim said *it's here*," Madeleine reminded him, "and it's not possible he's mistaken."

"Agreed," Doc said.

"So only one possibility remains," she surmised.

"Which is?" Doc asked.

"It must be smaller than you think," she reasoned. "Have you checked the closets?"

"Yeah, because I thought it might be behind a secret panel or something," he said.

"Wouldn't Jim have told you that?" Madeleine asked.

"Yeah, I guess so, but I was out of options," Doc admitted. "*That's why I asked you.*"

"Aha! The truth has finally begun to surface," she chuckled.

"You know what I mean." Doc tried to amend his slight. "You're good at this stuff."

"Have you looked under the beds?" Madeleine asked just to be thorough.

"That's not practical," Doc reasoned. "It must be anchored and easy to get open."

"So we've eliminated the impossible," Madeleine said. "And as I told you in Rome, what remains, no matter how improbable, must be the truth."

"Which is?" Doc pressed her.

"It's got to be anchored where you haven't looked that's easy to access," she concluded.

Doc then looked around with different eyes.

"Jim would put it in *this* room," he said and scanned it again and focused on the bar.

"Are you thinking what I'm thinking?" Madeleine asked with a playful smile.

Doc walked around the bar and looked underneath its broad mahogany counter.

"BINGO!" he said loudly when he spotted a steel drawer three-feet-wide and eight-inches-deep with a combination lock.

He spun the dial to the numbers Jim provided and the drawer slid open easily. Inside was a thick, oversized, black polymer pistol case with *CornerShot* molded into it.

"Anything interesting inside?" Madeleine asked.

"Not really." Doc lied because he didn't want to spend time discussing weapons with Q on the deck while everyone else was trying to relax.

"Well then, let's head upstairs and join the others," Madeleine said happily.

"I'm right behind you!" Doc said as he closed and locked the safe.

Up on the deck with the others, Doc settled into a chair between Connie and Q.

"Welcome back my beloved husband," Connie said, happy that he'd opted to relax and spend time with the group.

"You make it sound as though I've been gone a long time," he chuckled.

"Well, it seemed like a long time," Connie replied,

and sipped on the margarita Marsha had mixed for her. "Opportunities like this are rare. If you recall, the last time we attempted it in Montana, you and your pals soon ran off on a mission."

"Don't be too hard on me," Doc sighed. "That's the reason we're here now, enjoying this beautiful home with an incredible view of the ocean, and relaxing with a sea breeze."

"We're here because we can't go home at the moment, remember?" Connie said for the record. "Someone tried to kill us and you make this sound like we casually booked an all-inclusive oceanfront rental to get away from it all."

"You must learn to look on the bright side, Beauty," Doc said in an effort to keep the conversation light.

"The *bright side* is that whoever tried to kill us in Montana apparently doesn't know we're here," Connie summarized. "But you've managed to find others here who tried to kill you."

"You *have* been paying attention," Doc replied, still trying to keep it light.

"More than you know, my sweet man," Connie sighed. "More than you know."

"Well, I promise to try to do better," Doc said sincerely. "But duty does call."

"Sometimes I wish you'd change the number...or retire the phone," Connie said.

"Ahhh, there's that word again," Doc sighed.

"Which word?" Connie asked.

"*Retire*," Doc answered. "You know we're both retired...and at early ages."

"*Semi-retired, at best!*" Connie corrected him and took another sip of her drink. "And I'm not even sure that's true. How many semi-retired people do you know who do what you do?"

"My dear, just because we don't know about it doesn't mean it's not being done," Doc reminded her. "After all, that's the whole point, isn't it? And besides, you knew all this when we were still just dating."

"Well, you got me there," she conceded.

"And now I've got you here!" Doc said as he leaned her way, wrapped an arm around her shoulders, pulled her close, and kissed her affectionately. "So let's promise to enjoy the rest of our time here together."

"I promise if you do," Connie said and finished her drink with one last sip.

"I promise too," Doc replied.

"I'm going in for another drink," Connie said. "Would you like one?"

"No thanks, Beauty. I'm good," Doc answered.

"You're the best, John!" Connie caressed him affectionately and went inside.

"Well Doc, where did Madeleine find you?" Q asked.

"I was just checking out the basement," Doc said simply. "It's as nice as the upstairs."

"Did you hear back from Jim?" Q asked next.

"Yeah," Doc answered. "He was glad to hear we enjoyed ourselves with the XRail."

"When are they coming home?" Q asked.

"Tomorrow afternoon, actually," Doc said.

As Q was about to ask another question, he received a text on his phone.

"It's from Jim," Q said. "He says you're ignoring his texts and he wants to know if we found the CornerShot. What the hell is that?"

"When did you give him your number?" Doc asked with exasperation. "And I'm not ignoring his texts. I just turned my phone off to be able to relax with Connie and all of you, okay?"

"Well, don't get upset, Doc," Q said. "It was just a question. So what's a CornerShot?"

"You're hopeless," Doc sighed and got out of his chair. "Hey, Noah," he said. "Q and I are going downstairs for a minute. Care to join us?"

"Sure!" Noah replied. "What's up?"

"Jim texted us about a surprise he has for us in the basement," Doc said.

"Jim's as much an American as you two," Noah chuckled. "So if must be another gun."

"Let's go find out," Q replied and led the way.

"And where are you fellas going?" Connie asked as they walked through the kitchen.

"We'll just be in the basement for a few minutes," Doc assured her.

"Can I get that in writing?" she answered, only half-kidding.

In the lower family room, Doc opened the gun safe once again, laid the CornerShot case on the bar, and opened it.

"Well, this is something different!" Q noted the obvious. "What's it supposed to do?"

Noah opened the owner's manual and began reading.

"CornerShot is engineered for around-the-corner

observation and sniping," he read aloud. "It was invented by Lt. Col. Amos Golan of the Israeli Defense Forces for use by law enforcement agencies, SWAT teams, and Special Forces around the world in hostile situations, often involving terrorists and hostages. Similar to the periscope rifle, it allows operators to both see and attack armed targets without exposing the operators to counterattack."

"Jim told me my 45 caliber would fit in it," Doc recalled out loud. "So I'm going to go get it. Sit tight."

"What a strange expression," Noah said with a shake of the head as Doc went upstairs.

"Okay, boys. Let's see that contraption," Doc said as he pulled his Taurus PT111 from its holster.

Installation was simple. Doc turned the CornerShot on and marveled at how light the polymer device was.

"Now what?" he asked Noah.

"Hit the *On* switch and the LCD screen acts as a scope," Noah told him. "Then you can turn the pistol end 62 degrees to the left or right using the collapsible lever below the stock. Pull the lever again and the weapon snaps back to its straight configuration like a traditional weapon."

Doc squatted behind the bar and raised the weapon like a periscope to view the room on the LCD screen.

"This is an amazing invention!" he exclaimed, then tried the buttons that turned the flashlight, infrared light, and two aiming lasers on and off.

"So we're going back to the shooting range in the morning?" Q asked excitedly.

"Most definitely!" Doc replied with a smile.

"You Americans are a trip!" Noah chuckled and closed the manual.

"Speaking of trips," Doc said. "We'd better get back outside and spend time with our wives before they refuse to ever take another trip with us."

"Do you think they'd really do that?" Q asked with an impish smile.

"I know Madeleine would give it serious thought," Noah answered.

"And Connie would put it in writing," Doc added. "I think this mission has pushed her closer to her limit than any other. So I can't say that I blame her."

"It's comforting to know that one of you has a limit," Q quipped as they headed upstairs.

Chapter Twelve – An Impressive Piece of Engineering

The next morning Q, Doc, and Noah arrived at the gun range a half hour before it opened. Q examined the CornerShot the whole way there, while Doc drove and Noah savored an extra-large cup of hot coffee he made Doc stop at the Quikmart for, just a half mile from the house.

"So did you get Swiss Mocha?" Q asked with a sly grin.

"That's your best try at humor?" Noah asked sarcastically. "For your information, it's Dark Magic Extra-Bold. You should try it some time. I understand it makes people funnier."

"Well, it's not working for you this morning, Swiss boy!" Q poked fun at him some more.

"I thought the Swiss preferred English breakfast tea," Doc said, to interrupt them.

"Many do," Noah replied. "But I needed something much stronger this morning. I know the ladies enjoyed spending time with us and having some good laughs last night, but we wrapped it up way too late for me."

"You're a HEMA Grand Master, Noah!" Doc asserted. "Doesn't that require stamina?"

"Stamina, yes; insomnia, no!" Noah protested.

"So tell me what HEMA is about exactly," Q requested.

"Well, you saw the broadsword I brought with me on that mission to Acre, Israel, right?" Noah began. "Do you remember when that spirit Knight Templar told me to draw my sword, testing my resolve by challenging my will to use it?"

"Sure," Q answered. "That was a deadly piece of hardware."

"Twenty-eight pounds of hardened carbon steel, sharpened to a razor edge and three feet long," Noah added. "It takes both hands and every muscle in your body to wield it. That's why it's still the most popular weapon among devotees of the historic European martial arts."

"Why swordfight when you can use a gun?" Q asked earnestly.

"Why use a gun when you can take your time terrifying and humiliating an enemy while preparing to kill him?" Noah asked just as earnestly.

"And all this time I feared you were a pacifist!" Q said with a chuckle and a sigh of relief.

"I am when I can afford to be," Noah replied. "But with life on the line, I'm a pragmatist."

"Well, that's mighty good to know," Q told him.

Doc saw the sign in the window of the gun range office get flipped to *OPEN* and exited his rental extended cab, four-wheel-drive pickup.

"You fellas come along as soon as you finish talking about being manly," he jabbed away at them.

"We're right behind you, Doc!" Q said as he rolled out of his side with the CornerShot.

"I'm going first this time!" Noah shouted.

"Well, listen to the swordfighter," Q chuckled.

"I wouldn't rag him too much about that if I were you, Q," Doc cautioned. "He just might challenge you to cross broadswords with him. Believe me, it's a workout. And that Stetson of yours won't protect you."

"I'm always up for a little exercise," Q replied, flexing his arm muscles.

Doc silently shook his head and smiled. He knew that, sooner or later, the time would come for Q's first FEMA lesson, and the former Navy SEAL looked forward to being there for it.

"Okay, you first, Noah," Doc said. "And remember that because of the angle of fire this weapon will kick sideways instead of back or upward. Fire when ready."

Noah took his time getting oriented to using the LED screen to sight the weapon, then fired off a half dozen rounds, the last four of which hit the target within a three-inch spread.

"Excellent job, my friend!" Doc shouted.

"I gotta give all the credit to this screen," Noah said. "This is an impressive piece of engineering alright!"

"Just imagine being able to shoot around corners with that much accuracy," Q noted. "How great would it be to get the drop on the enemy when he can't even see you?"

"That's the point of this weapon," Doc added. "It makes it possible to see around corners, over barriers, even under cars—and shoot with accuracy if you must—without exposing yourself to enemy fire. From now on," he declared, "we'll have at least one of these handy on every mission."

"My turn!" Q called out and loaded a full clip into the 1911.

He lifted the CornerShot in the air as if looking over a wall, and fired all eight rounds.

"I gotta get me one of these!" Q said with a satisfied grin. "I agree with you, Doc, about having one with us at all times. Same goes for the XRail. Add in our handguns and a couple of good long-range rifles and we'll be ready for just about any situation."

"Roger that!" Doc said. "I knew we had to have come all this way and met Jim Danforth for a mighty good reason. And now I'm so glad we did."

Doc was last to fire the CornerShot and was equally convinced of its usefulness. The trio each took two more turns with the weapon before Doc put it back in its case. Then they headed back to Sugar Tree. During the ride back, thoughts of home were on everyone's mind.

"We'll definitely always have room in the trunk and gun safe for a couple of these," he declared. "I'll order two—and two XRails—when we get back to Montana, which hopefully will be soon."

"That's a mighty fine place you have out there, Doc," Q told him. "But it wouldn't be at all bad to spend summers down here. Are you giving it any thought? I certainly am."

"Since you brought it up, I plan to talk with Connie about it later today," Doc said.

"Well keep me posted," Q said, "because I'm sure going to talk with Marsha about it."

"I'm pretty sure you can count me and Madeleine in too," Noah said. "She loves it here and I know she'd really love to spend more time with Connie and Marsha."

"If you get a place down here will ya bring those swords with you?" Q poked at him.

"Oh, here we go again!" Doc interjected. "I'm warning you, Q, you're playing with fire."

"I'm a big boy," Q chuckled.

"Laugh while you can, old man," Noah said from the back seat. "When we get back to Sugar Tree you best not push me or I'll give you your first lesson."

"Lesson in what? HEMA?" Q chuckled sarcastically.

"In HEMA...and in humility!" Noah quietly corrected him.

"You know, you talk awfully tough for a guy from Switzerland," Q jabbed some more.

"What's that supposed to mean?" Noah asked with a grin.

"I thought you were all peace-loving folks," Q poked some more.

"Didn't your President Reagan always say, 'Peace through strength'?" Noah asked.

"Now *there* was an *American*!" Q said.

"Same goes for the Swiss Army," Noah declared.

"Switzerland has an army?" Q kept poking.

"Take it easy, Q, before you talk yourself into a real corner," Doc chuckled.

"How about the Swiss Guard of the Vatican?" Noah asked. "Does that ring a bell?"

"Okay, okay," Q finally relented. "I'll give you that... but no one's ever going to attack the Vatican. So they almost don't count."

"That does it!" Noah finally called Q's bluff. "Get ready for your first lesson when we get back to Sugar Tree. We'll do it out on the beach. The sand will almost make it a fair fight."

"Well, you two tough guys will have to wait just a little longer because I'm going to stop at the gun shop for a few minutes," Doc informed them.

"What for this time?" Q asked.

"I want to buy some rock salt shells and see how the XRail handles them tomorrow before we pick up Anne and Jim at the airport," Doc said.

"Rock salt?" Noah asked. "Why rock salt?"

"It's non-lethal except at very close range, but it sends your target the message that you mean business," Doc explained.

"Who do you plan to send a message to?" Q asked. "Do you know something we don't?"

"No, nothing like that," Doc assured him. "But you know I prefer not to kill and I'd just like to fire some salt shells to see how the XRail handles 'em. I should have done that yesterday. But I didn't think of it until now for some reason."

"Well *that* certainly makes me nervous," Q said.

"Why is that?" Doc asked.

"*Because everything happens for a reason*!" Q and Noah both answered, and laughed.

"Laugh if you want to, you two," Doc responded. "But you both have been around me enough—and seen enough—to know it's true!"

Doc was paying for the shells at the gun shop when his cell phone rang.

"Hello, Chief!" he said to Chief Russell Trapp. "I hope this is just a courtesy call."

"I wish it were," the chief said. "Are you and your group still in the area?"

"I have a sneaking suspicion you already know the answer to that, Chief," Doc replied. "But yes, we expect to be here at least another couple of days. Why do you ask?"

"Well, to be honest with you, I've been unable to convince the Byrnes brothers to head back to Arizona where they belong. Instead, they've insisted on sticking around—and nosing around—the entire week of their so-called vacation. I've got them on extensions listening in right now and they refused to leave me alone until I contacted you."

"Hello, Mr. Holiday!" Tom piped up.

"Hi, Mr. Holiday!" Raymon said too.

"Hello, fellas," Doc replied to both of them. "You boys stick around much longer and you're going to have a

Georgia accent when you finally get back to the Valentine State."

"Nobody calls it the Valentine State, Mr. Holiday!" Raymon informed Doc.

"And no one who knows me calls me Mr. Holiday," Doc said. "So be nice and just call me Doc. Okay?"

"Okay, Doc!" Raymon said. "And please call me Ray... and call my brother Tom."

"Now we're talking," Doc chuckled. "Do you just miss me, or do you have something you want to discuss?"

"We fear you and your team are still in danger, Doc," Tom told him. "We've spent the past couple of days enjoying the nightlife and watering holes around the area and best we can tell there are still a number of Guardians in the area, and very unhappy about your team having put a halt to their operation...which we understand was the recovery of a nuclear device, is that right?"

"Can't discuss it with you, fellas," Doc said abruptly. "Sorry, but it does make sense that there are more here than the four we apprehended. Do you know how many?"

"At least twelve, maybe more" Tom replied. "They've been lying low, hoping the four you had locked up might be released. But when they drink, they start flappin' their jaws and telling each other what they are going to do to you if and when they find you. According to all that we heard last night in a brew pub on the north end of Tybee Island, they believe they know where you're at and they plan to settle the score."

"Well, I certainly appreciate your letting me know, Tom," Doc said. "We're headed back to where we're staying right now, and we'll be on the lookout for trouble."

"I must insist that my department get involved, Doc," the chief interrupted. "We can't let you face this alone and endanger our locals in the process. Are you still at the Danforth place? I can have several officers there in minutes."

"We are, Chief," Doc replied. "But I know you agree that this needs to be kept as low-key as possible. There's no need to alarm the Danforths' neighbors unnecessarily...especially while they're away."

"Actually, I'm glad to hear they're not in harm's way," the chief answered. "I'll lead four officers in two unmarked cars and quietly pull into that monster garage he has, if you make sure someone opens the garage doors when we arrive."

"We're headed there now, Chief," Doc said. "I'll alert our wives to watch for you and your men. Talk to you when we get there. And thanks for your support on this, Tom and Ray. We owe you big time."

"It's our pleasure, Doc," Tom said.

"Glad to help!" Raymon added.

"See you soon, Doc," the chief said, and ended the call.

"Fellas, we gotta get back to Sugar Tree *now*!" Doc told his partners, grabbed the three boxes of rock salt shells, and led the charge back to the truck.

"What's up?" Q asked as Doc squealed the tires pulling away from the gun shop.

"Call Marsha and tell her and Connie and Madeleine to batten down the hatches. Tell them Chief Trapp and his men will arrive shortly in two unmarked cars and will need to park them in the garage, out of sight."

"Holy crap!" Noah shouted in the back seat. "What now?!"

"The Byrnes brothers happened to overhear what sounded to them like a plot to ambush us today by Guardians we didn't know about."

While Q was on the phone with Marsha, Doc punched the speed dial for Jim Danforth on his own phone and handed it to Noah.

"When Jim answers, explain the situation as best you can," Doc told him.

While Noah and Q passed the word, Doc raced the truck back to Skidaway Island and Sugar Tree. As he wheeled the pickup into the garage beside the unmarked police cars, Q and Noah ended their calls.

"Jim said he and Anne, Louis, and Jenny are catching the next flight back," Noah said.

"I've got a better idea," Doc replied as they exited the truck. "Call him back and tell him to go directly to Fairchild Air Force Base. I'll call President Preston and arrange to have them flown directly here by the fastest means possible. And the President will clear things with Louis and Jenny's COs too."

"Will do!" Noah said as he jogged into the house behind Q and Doc.

"Thank God you're home safe and sound!" Connie said, and wrapped her arms around Doc. "What's the plan? You always have a plan."

"Honestly, Beauty, it just seems that way," Doc replied.

"But I do think there might be a safe way to handle this with a minimum of disruption to the neighborhood."

"Disruption to the neighborhood?!" the chief loudly echoed with doubt. "Do you understand what could be about to happen here?"

"I believe I do, Chief," Doc answered. "Noah, toss me my phone please."

Doc caught the phone with his right hand while holding Connie close with his left arm.

"Hello, Mr. President," Doc said, a heartbeat after hitting the White House speed-dial icon. "We're in a code red here on Skidaway Island. We've learned that a handful of Guardians are still on the loose and they plan to ambush us soon. So we would appreciate it if you could order Commander Broadmore to have a couple of his cutters five or six miles off the north end of Skidaway Island pronto. Have him call me as soon as he's in place and I'll advise him of the situation and the plan."

"I'll do it right now, Doc," the President said. "Please be careful, but do whatever's necessary to keep everyone safe!"

"Roger that, Mr. President. Talk to you soon!" Doc responded, and ended the call.

11

THE BATTLE BEGINS

Awaiting the Guardians' arrival gave Doc time to slow down and think more clearly.

"I see you brought your Arizona Auxiliary with you," Doc said to the chief with a grin, and nodded to Tom and Raymon, who were standing quietly in opposite corners of the living room. "Welcome to the team."

"They're acting as observers only," the chief assured Doc. "Ain't that right, boys?"

"Sure is, Chief," Tom said in a tone that sounded practiced.

"The more I think about it the more I believe we should have parked bumper-to-bumper on the circular drive in front to act as a barrier," he told Doc, who was sitting at the next window.

"I don't think they'll hit us from the front, Chief," Doc answered.

"I believe you're right, Doc," Q said. "They don't want to attract attention any more than we do."

"So what *are* you thinkin'?" the chief asked as he tipped his hat back and rocked back in his chair.

"My best guess is that they'll hit us as it begins to get dark and the tide is in," Doc said as he looked out a nearby window toward the ocean. "If I wanted to do this as quietly as possible, I'd come by boat, drop anchor about 100 feet out, and wade ashore to have the advantage of surprise."

"So what's your plan?" the chief asked.

"Hear me out on this before you shut me down, okay?" Doc asked.

"Okay, but just this once," the Chief said as he rubbed his forehead.

"For starters, I'm asking you and your men to stand down unless things get out of control," Doc said. "I know that makes you nervous. But I believe there's a way to repel this bunch with a minimum of conflict and send them right into the waiting arms of the Coast Guard. That would avoid the Danforths' home being shot to pieces and minimize the chance that any nearby residents will even suspect anything's going on. It will hopefully also result in all the Guardians being alive for questioning. Right now we need all the info we can get out of them."

"You're not good for my ulcer," the chief told Doc as he rubbed his belly.

"Welcome to my world," Q told the chief sarcastically.

"Mine too!" Noah added with a laugh. "But he keeps things from getting boring."

"What's wrong with boring?" the chief asked, only

half in jest. "We get pretty used to it around here most of the year."

Doc's phone rang again. It was Commander Broadmore.

"I've got two cutters holding their position six nautical miles off shore and waiting for your signal to close in and take the Guardians into custody if they try to escape by sea."

"Thanks for the fast response, Commander," Doc said. "Stand by...and keep your eyes peeled for Guardians in your vicinity. You may well see them before we do."

"Aye-aye, Doc!" the commander replied. "Standing by on orders from the President of the United States."

"Roger that!" Doc said with new comfort, and ended the call. "Chief, I'd appreciate it if you would have two of your officers in a couple of the front windows just in case I'm wrong about how this all goes down."

"You heard him men!" the chief said. "Tom and Ray, you are now on special assignment with the Tybee Island Police Department. So man the front windows."

"Will do, Chief!" Tom replied, and moved to the front of the house with Raymon.

"I'll take my officers up to the second floor for a bird's eye view of the surroundings, front and back," the chief told Doc. "But first, let's talk about the details of your so-called plan, Doc. How do you plan to pull this off, exactly?"

"Well, I don't want any of the Guardians to reach the house," Doc began. "That's why I'm hoping I'm right about their arriving in boats. If and when they do, Q and

Noah and I will be ready for them with XRail shotguns. Are you familiar with them, Chief?"

"Isn't that a semi-automatic, twenty-five-round shotgun?" the chief asked.

"Exactly!" Doc replied. "We'll load each of them with three chambers worth of rock salt shells, and load the fourth chamber with live rounds. Hopefully, the three of us emptying three chambers of rock salt each will convince them to turn and run. If not, we'll have to resort to doing things the more traditional way. But someone hit by a 12-gauge shotgun shell usually doesn't do too much talking afterward, if you know what I mean."

"Hardly ever," the chief said with a shake of his head.

"Here we are in the deep south, stuck in a situation right out of the old west," Q noted.

"Not if we can help it," Doc answered. "If we do repel them back into their boats, Commander Broadmoor will close in and take them into custody. Then they'll be all yours, Chief," Doc said.

"Who do you think you're kidding?" the chief asked incredulously. "The Feds will be crawling all over this place and I'll be lucky to get a question in edgewise."

"I fear you may be right," Doc answered. "But we'll take it one step at a time until then. I need a couple of your officers to take Connie, Madeleine, and Marsha to the station, where they'll be safe, just in case things get out of hand here."

"We want to stay here with all of you, John," Connie announced.

"I know you all do," Doc replied. "But it will be best if

we know that the three of you are safe if things go sideways here."

"Please be careful!" Connie came to Doc and said. "Is there anything Marsha and Madeleine and I can do before we go?"

"We've made more than enough lunch for everyone," Madeleine announced. "Who wants some? You all may as well eat while you can."

"I'm ready to eat!" Q chimed in.

"You're always ready!" Marsha laughed.

"And so are you, Noah!" Madeleine jumped in and joined in the first laughter since the police arrived.

"You're on your own, boys! Don't forget to clean up after yourselves!" Marsha said with a smile as she followed the officers to the garage along with Connie and Madeleine.

"Do your best, be safe, and see you soon!" Connie called out, and fell in line to the garage.

"Do be careful, all of you!" Madeleine said, and closed the door to the garage behind her.

"We will!" the men called out with a practiced smile, and waved goodbye.

Everyone ate lunch at the windows. Doc, Q, and Noah loaded the rock salt and ammo into Jim's three XRails, then exchanged small talk with the others for the next couple of hours, while they watched for suspicious movement outside. Then, just as the sun neared the horizon, Doc got the call he'd been anticipating from Commander Broadmore.

"You've got three speedboats headed your way with what looks to be about six men in each," the commander told him. "You should be able to see them any minute now."

"Okay, Commander," Doc replied. "Close in behind them about 100 yards off shore, until we know whether they're headed back your way, or I need you and your men ashore."

"Aye-aye, Doc!" the commander shot back.

Noah now had the Guardians' boats in sight.

"We definitely have company!" he called out to the others. "They're headed right here."

Doc jumped to Noah's window for a good look.

"Showtime!" Doc announced. "Q, I want you behind a few of the Adirondack chairs up on the second-floor deck," he said. "Noah and I will take positions just under the sugar trees at the back of the property. We'll let them step off into the surf, but open up on them as they start to wade ashore. Don't fire until Noah and we do. But once you start, empty all three rock salt chambers right through the tops of the trees. When seventy-five rounds of painful rock salt rains down on them from three directions, they won't have any idea how many shooters they're up against.

"Hopefully, that'll be enough to persuade them to turn around and head back out to sea and into the arms of the Coast Guard. If it doesn't, I'll give you the signal and all three of us will unleash live ammo on them. If it comes to that, the Coasties will close in from behind on what's left of them, which should bring this to an end."

"Chief, if and when we resort to live ammo, feel free to take whatever actions you deem necessary to help us end this," Doc said. "God willing, it won't come to that and the Coasties will have them in custody before you break a sweat."

"Sounds good to me, Doc," the chief replied. "I really expect they'll turn and run when they feel that rock salt hit them."

"Well, we're about to find out," Doc replied, and led Noah out the back door and into the thick stand of fifteen-foot sugar trees.

Q could hear the faint sound of the Guardians' boats approaching as he pulled two Adirondack chairs together at the railing overlooking the back of the property, and crouched behind them. He slid the XRail's blunt barrel between the chairs and watched Doc and Noah disappear into the shade of the thick trees. The sun was at their backs and began to dip below the horizon as the boats of the Guardians closed in.

"Hold steady, Noah," Doc said quietly. "They have no idea we know they're coming. Let them all step into the water. It will slow their reaction time and we'll have the drop on them and pelt them good as they scramble to get back into the boats."

"That makes much more sense than, 'Don't shoot until you see the whites of their eyes,'" Noah joked to relieve his tension.

"I'll be thrilled if we never see the whites of their eyes, Noah...just the white in their panicked faces as they turn and run," Doc replied.

As the boats slowed in the water, Tom and Ray intently watched the front of the house for any frontal assault. Chief Trapp and his officers had a perfect view of the waterfront action from the first-floor rear windows. Q crouched and laid his index finger on the trigger of his XRail on the sundeck and Doc and Noah braced for themselves for the well-laid counter assault about to erupt as the Guardians dropped their anchors and began climbing out of the boats.

Doc softly counted the Guardians as they stepped into the water.

"One, two, three, four, five," he counted, and noted they all wore tactical military-grade combat boots. "Six, seven, eight, nine..." He counted with trepidation as he saw they all carried Swiss-made SIG AMT automatic rifles. "These are not ragtag thugs, Noah," he said. "It would be best if they don't have a chance to return fire. They're carrying the best weapon your country has produced. Hopefully, they're not as well-trained as they are well-equipped."

"We'll know as soon as the fire and fury rains down on 'em," Noah whispered.

The Guardians were now all thigh-deep in the surf and just steps from the shore.

"FIRE!" Doc shouted as he squeezed and held the trigger of his XRail.

The XRails performed flawlessly! Three raging, deadly shotguns each blasted two shells full of rock salt pellets per second at the unsuspecting Guardians for more than thirty heart-stopping seconds! The un-battle-tested, gun-shy brigade panicked, screamed, and twisted in pain as the rock salt rained down on them like flesh-piercing hail. Their muscles cramped and their bodies contorted as they slogged like stiff-legged zombies with spasms through the thigh-high water.

"Holy shit, they're going to kill us all!" one of them yelled to the others.

"Get out of my way, idiot, before I shoot you!" a distinctly female voice shouted.

Desperately and clumsily, the terrified Guardians all scrambled over one another to get back into the three anchored boats that rocked and swayed in the surf as Commander Broadmore and his pair of heavily armed Coast Guard cutters bore down on them.

"The Keeper can go to hell!" a Guardian shouted. "I didn't sign on for this shit!"

When it was clear the Guardians were on the run and not returning fire, Q rose to his feet on the sundeck and fired his remaining rock salt shells at them for good measure.

"Hoooo yeahhhhh!" he shouted as his nostrils filled with the smell of gun powder.

"This is the United States Coast Guard!" Commander Broadmore shouted at them over the loudspeaker. "You are all under arrest! I want all of you in in the water NOW! Throw your weapons into the water and raise your hands where I can see them OR YOU WILL BE SHOT! Shout 'Yes' if you can hear me and you understand me!"

"Yes!" the Guardians all shouted.

The few Guardians who had managed to climb into their boats all got back in the water. The M2 50-caliber machine guns mounted and manned on the bow of each cutter were deadly proof that the commander was serious. The monster guns' armor-piercing shells could destroy a concrete block wall at 150 yards. So the

Guardians had no doubt their fiberglass boats would be disintegrated at just thirty feet away.

When the commander was sure all the Guardians were in sight and in the water, he read them their Miranda Rights before taking them aboard.

"You have the right to remain silent and refuse to answer questions," he shouted loud and clear while an Ensign videotaped the onboarding process. "Anything you say may be used against you in a court of law. You have the right to consult an attorney before speaking to the police and to have an attorney present during questioning, now or in the future. Is that clear?"

"Yes!" the Guardians all shouted.

"Now line up single file an arm's length apart and we will assist you aboard one at a time," the commander barked at them. "One false move, one look away from this cutter will result in your being shot! If you resist being brought aboard, you will be shot! If you do not follow our orders upon boarding, you will be shot! Do you understand?"

"Yes!" the Guardians all shouted.

"I wonder if the commander has teenagers at home," Doc said to Noah with a grin as the two of them stepped out from under the sugarberry trees, into the fast-fading sunlight.

At the water's edge, Doc turned and looked back at the few other oceanfront homes that were visible and he didn't see anyone in the windows or on the beach. He hoped that meant there would be a minimum of 911 calls from frightened and/or angry residents. The last thing he wanted was for the Danforths to come home to upset neighbors. Doc smiled and laughed to himself because the thought brought back high school memories of trying to discretely have friends at the house while his parents were away on short trips. Doc chuckled and hoped this operation was more successful than any of those.

"What's so funny?" Noah asked.

"Oh, I'm just hoping we managed to pull off the biggest, most dangerous event in the island's history without a single neighbor being aware of it," Doc replied.

"Well, I'm sure the Danforths will appreciate that," Noah said.

"Yep!" Doc agreed. "I just had to laugh with relief when that very thought came to mind. I'd hate for them to regret having been kind enough to let us stay here while they were away. But at the same time, I think we owe them a clear understanding of how important this operation may prove to be...and how their act of kindness made it possible."

"I want to be there when you try to put that in perspective for them while you downplay the event we just pulled off," Noah told him with a sly grin.

"You and Q *both* better be there," Doc said. "I'll need help choosing the right words."

Doc and Noah watched the last Guardians being lifted from the water, hauled aboard, and handcuffed at the stern of the commander's cutter. Just moments after all sixteen were in custody, Doc's cell phone rang with a call from the President.

"Great work, Doc!" the President bellowed into the phone.

Doc jerked the phone from his ear and Noah heard

the President as though Doc had turned on his speakerphone.

"You got 'em all in custody without a lethal shot being fired! You and your team are amazing! I can't thank the three of you enough, on behalf of myself and the entire nation!"

"There were far more men involved in the success of this operation, Mr. President," Doc advised him. "First and foremost, Commander Broadmore and his crewmen coordinated with us perfectly. So did Tybee Island Police Chief Russell Trapp and his officers. The same goes for FBI Special Agent Tom Byrnes and his brother Ray Byrnes, a Maricopa County deputy sheriff."

"So noted, Doc!" the President told him.

"Mr. President, I'd really appreciate a chance to talk with you briefly tomorrow about things we've learned and things we believe to be true."

"And you will, Doc," the President said. "I'll call you at noon tomorrow. Doc, I just got word that the Danforth family has arrived at the Hunter Army Airfield. They're being driven to their home by motorcade and will arrive in the next twenty minutes."

Chief Trapp stepped in close to Doc and said, "Ask him to tell the motorcade that I'll have two unmarked squad cars waiting at the intersection of North Landings Way and Priest Landing Drive. We can make the transfer there and transport Jim Danforth and his family quietly through the neighborhood so as not to alarm area residents."

"Did you hear that, Mr. President?" Doc asked and handed his phone to the chief.

"I did. They're being advised as we speak," the President answered. "Thanks, Chief Trapp, for the strong support. Great job by the way! Very sorry that I can't thank you publicly, but if you will send me the names of the personnel involved, I'll have letters of commendation prepared for their files. How's that?"

"That's very kind of you, Mr. President," the chief said sincerely. "Thank you on behalf of my entire department!"

"And THANK YOU, Chief, on behalf of the entire nation!" the President bellowed, and ended the call.

"And to think I didn't vote for the man!" the chief said with wide eyes as he handed Doc his phone back.

"Well, you'll have a chance to do so when he runs for re-election," Doc chuckled.

12

BACK AT SQUARE ONE

Twenty minutes later, the Danforth clan returned to Sugar Tree and could only guess all that must have gone on in their absence.

"Welcome home!" Doc, Connie, and the rest of the team shouted with open arms.

"It's great to be home!" Anne Danforth said, and group-hugged with Connie, Marsha, and Madeleine.

"Don't leave me out!" Jenny said loudly, and inserted herself into the hug. "I'm part of the family now, you know."

"Yes, we know and we're so very happy for you and Louis!" Connie said. "Let me introduce everyone! Q, Marsha, Noah, and Madeleine, these are our newest friends, Jim and Anne and Louis and Jenny. I'll leave it to you all to sort out the last names," she laughed.

"So did anything exciting happen while we were away?" Jim asked with a sly grin, because he really had no clue of the events that had just transpired in the short time his family was in Spokane.

"A thing or two," Doc said coyly. "But you go first. How was the wedding?"

"It was magnificent!" Anne shouted excitedly and hugged Jenny. "I am so pleased and proud to have Jenny in the family. I told my son she was a catch the day Jim and I met her."

"Really?" Jenny asked. "I never knew that."

"Well, it's true," Jim confirmed. "And I'm hoping I don't have to wait too long to be a proud grandpa!"

"That's a whole other conversation," Anne advised him. "In fact, I'm not sure it involves any conversation at all."

"Um, folks, can we change the subject?" Louis good-naturedly chimed in. "Or better yet, can we get something to eat?"

"You bet!" Marsha said loudly. "I've got the oven preheating and Connie and Madeleine picked up what look like delicious half-baked pizzas at the local market...and several large bottles of wine. I hope that's okay with everyone."

"*Absolutely!*" was the group's response.

The group retreated to the large dining room to get comfortable, open the wine, and get to know one another while waiting for the pizzas.

"So, Jenny," Connie was bursting to ask, "what's the status for you and Louis having to report for duty?"

"The most unexpected thing happened," Jenny said with a smile as she glanced at her new husband and he handed her a folded piece of paper from his shirt pocket. "We got this telegram delivered by military courier at our reception advising us that we've both been temporarily assigned to something called 'a local special services group with operations here in the greater Savannah area, Northwest Montana, and other classified locations.'"

"Welcome aboard, you two!" Doc said with a big smile. "I'd requested as much before you left for Spokane. I guess in all the excitement, he forgot to confirm his decision with me."

"Well thanks, Doc!" Louis said in a way that sounded like he'd guessed it early on.

"Don't be too quick with your thanks, Louis," Doc told him. "The President's in the habit of getting the most out of his decisions. You can bet you'll both earn this time together."

"That's fine with us," Jenny assured him. "We'd appreciate a couple of days of R and R, but then we'll be ready for anything."

"I'll hold you to that," Doc said with another smile.

"What about Anne and me?" Jim asked, half serious. "We're retired, not dead."

"Hush, James Robert!" Anne good-naturedly scolded him. "Your days of high adventure have long been over with...and good riddance!"

"Well, he could have fooled me, in the crazy rocket boat of his!" Q said boldly.

"What on earth is he talking about, Jim?" Anne asked and took another sip of wine.

"Nothin' important, darlin'," Jim drawled meekly. "I just took the boys out for a short joy ride before we left for the wedding."

The beep sounded, indicating the oven was ready for the pizzas.

"Saved by the bell!" Jim joked.

Marsha and the rest of the wives converged on the kitchen and were soon laughing as though they had known one another for years.

"It's damned good to be home," Jim sighed, sat back in his chair, and drained his wine glass. "Thanks for taking such good care of it, fellas. The place looks terrific. And the best Louis and I could tell from what little we gathered from the police, you had your hands full here with some characters out for blood."

"I'd say that's a pretty good estimation," Q replied with a smile and a sip of wine.

"We did our utmost to protect the home front," Noah added. "It's what we do best."

"And you do a great job," Jim answered with a satisfied grin. "I'm assuming those in the know believe the danger is passed, or they never would have brought us home. Am I right?"

"Best anyone can tell, Jim!" Doc replied. "But to be honest, I don't believe we can be sure of anything at this stage."

"What do you mean?" Louis asked.

"We're learning more each day about the number and resources of the Guardians, and the picture is growing grimmer, not brighter."

"How so?" Jim asked.

"I'm not at liberty to share everything I'm thinking before I report it to the President tomorrow. *What I can tell you* is that when we first got here, we thought we were just up against three Guardians in a small rented speed-boat. But now there are twenty in custody, and no one is sure we have all of them. And that's just here in the Savannah area. Best we can tell, no other local writers have been murdered. But they're dropping like flies elsewhere. And if we're right about their need to raise money to keep this insane murder ring well-financed, then you can bet they're up to no good somewhere else in the world as we speak."

"It does sound grim," Jim said quietly, and poured himself a little more wine. "I'm glad I'm not the one who has to crack this and bring it to a halt. But by God, I do believe you fellas are the right men for the job. Be sure to take good care of my daughter and son-in-law as you get it done, though, would ya? If you bring 'em back in better shape than when you found 'em—like you did our home —Anne and I will be eternally grateful."

"As I said, it's what we do," Noah replied.

Doc almost wished Noah hadn't made it sound so certain. But at the same time, he was gratified to hear the young swordsman from Switzerland speak with confidence against such unknown odds. It was a bold enough statement to carry Noah through the days and perils ahead. And Doc knew all too well the value and power of confidence in overcoming the dangers they could expect to confront before this mission was over.

"So what's next, Doc?" Louis asked.

"I'll know more after speaking with the President tomorrow," he replied. "But for now, I expect to be headed back to Montana to regroup and let the folks with a higher pay grade figure out where we go from here...if anywhere."

"But the President obviously thinks there's more to

do, or he wouldn't have arranged for Jenny and me to work with you," Louis reasoned.

"That's for certain," Doc agreed. "But the secret to our success in this profession is to not get too far ahead of the decision-makers. Believe me, that would be a no-win proposition."

"You can say that again," Q agreed. "So tomorrow we pack up and head west for some rest—and hopefully some fishin'—after you talk to the President," Q said happily.

"Noah, I'm sure you remember how I showed how to clean and oil the XRails," Doc said.

"I do!" Noah said, sounding as though he'd be happy to handle the guns one more time.

"I'll help," Louis volunteered. "It'll give us time to get to know one another. I don't even know where you're from. What's that accent I hear?"

"He's from another planet!" Q couldn't resist saying. "But he's okay just the same."

"American women do say I'm out of this world," Noah shot back.

"Don't let Madeleine hear you talk like that," Q replied. "She'll take you back to Europe."

"No way, Q," Noah gave his ready answer. "She'd never miss a chance to return to Montana. So you can't get rid of us that easy."

"I can see Jenny and I have a lot to learn about the six of you," Louis said.

"Hopefully, you'll get that chance amidst the peace and quiet of Flathead Lake over the next few days," Doc said optimistically, and became the next to drain his wine glass.

"Pizzas are ready!" Marsha shouted from the kitchen. "Come and get it!"

Everyone filled paper plates with pizza, refilled their wine glasses, and trailed out onto the large deck off the dining room to enjoy each other's company for a few peaceful hours that balmy evening, under a clear night sky filled with stars, and the sound of the ocean as it stroked the shore.

Doc did his very best to be in the moment, to enjoy good conversation with the best of friends. But Connie had seen the look in his eyes enough times to know his mind was bouncing between the conversations on the deck and the likely mission ahead. She didn't fault him for it. She loved him for it, because his love of country was stronger than his love of relaxation and small talk. There were times when she wished it wasn't so. But she'd learned early on that it always would be so. It made Doc who he was, the man and his commitment to service to the nation that she had fallen in love with.

Doc's mind was indeed bouncing between the friendly conversations on the deck at Sugar Tree and the serious talk he'd scheduled with the President that he needed to prepare for. That evening, Doc had no idea how to tell the President his feelings about his team's continued involvement in the hunt for Guardians of the Forbidden Library, as they were now known in intelligence circles around the world.

By sheer chance, and dumb luck, Doc and his team had learned some things about this new terrorist group and their international game of cat and mouse. He and his team had risked their lives and made only a tiny, local dent in what appeared to be a very large global organization. As far as he could tell, no one had a clue where—and whom—the Guardians would strike next.

The more law enforcement learned about the group, the less they knew. So now, after much effort, risk, and sacrifice, they were essentially back at square one. And Doc hated that feeling!

"What are you going to say to the President tomorrow, John?" Connie asked gently as they pulled the covers up to their chins and turned out the lights for the night.

"I really don't know, Beauty," he sighed. "He knows my heart's in this fight, as always. But I've got you and the rest of the team to think about. We've laid eyes on a few members of the Guardians. But most of the time I feel like we're chasing ghosts. To make matters worse, for the first time since I met him, I feel the President's not telling me everything he knows."

"Why do you say that?" Connie asked with surprise.

"He simply must know more," Doc reasoned. "The international intelligence community has been working on this night and day for months. We've stumbled our way around one small geographic area for just a few days and learned more than the President has shared with me, and he gets intelligence briefings first thing every morning. Don't you agree that he must know more about this than we do?"

"It would seem that way," Connie agreed. "But if he does, he must have good reasons not to share it with you."

"I prefer to believe that's the case," Doc said. "But that

doesn't change the fact that I'm leading this team into harm's way thinking that the President isn't being totally open with us."

"Do you honestly think he would knowingly set you up for failure?" Connie asked.

"I don't want to think that, Beauty," Doc said. "But I feel I have to tell the President that a lot more of the dots we have identified have to be connected *before* our team can effectively help to make any more connections."

"You plan to tell the President you won't help?" Connie asked with eyebrows raised.

"I plan to tell him our team must be equal partners with the other teams to have any hope for success." Doc measured his words carefully. "Our effectiveness hinges on the information we have as much as it does on our skills and experience. And we need to be certain we have all the information there is if we are to continue with any hope of success. Without it, we're taking unnecessary risks and wasting lots of money and precious time."

"Well, sleep on it, Honey," Connie told him, then hugged him and kissed him goodnight. "I'm sure you'll have the right words by the time you're speaking with him. You always do."

"Thanks, Beauty," Doc said and returned her kiss. "Goodnight my love."

Connie's words were exactly what Doc needed to sleep soundly. And he did.

13

WE'VE NEVER FAILED YET

Everyone awoke early the next morning, then packed and prepared for their flight to Montana. By the time of the President's call precisely at noon, they had finished a leisurely breakfast, washed the dishes, and set their luggage on the front porch.

"Hello again, Doc!" the President's usual cheerful voice boomed through the phone. "I hope everyone is rested and ready for the flight this afternoon. I've arranged to have you flown from Hunter Army Air Field to Fairchild Air Force Base outside Spokane. You'll board a chopper there that will set you down right in front of your house. Two SUVs should arrive shortly to pick you all up. By the way, I've been advised that your lawn has been repaired."

"Sounds good, Mr. President," Doc replied. "But I have some questions for you regarding what is now known about the Guardians."

"Ask away, Doc," the President said without hesitation. "I've set fifteen minutes aside for this call in case we needed it."

"For starters, do you have any idea how many there are, what cities they're in, and what they're likely to be mixed up in next?" Doc asked. "Have more writers or artists died?"

"INTERPOL estimates the likely number to be around 6,000 worldwide," the President said. "Scotland Yard is investigating what originally appeared to be a case of murder/suicide involving a writer and his artist girl-friend outside London two days ago. Same M.O. we're so familiar with now. A couple of seemingly unimportant items are missing. They haven't shared what they are yet. But we expect to have the complete story from them as soon as they realize the scenario we've shared with them is not a hair-brained conspiracy theory after all."

"How did they estimate the size of the group?" Doc asked.

"The FBI and INTERPOL canvased random tattoo parlors across the U.S. and Western Europe for a sample of how many have done 'Guardian' wrist tattoos," the President reported. "Frankly, I suspect the group is much larger. They know we're on to them. So it's likely they're being tattooed by fellow members, not by pro tattoo artists."

"You can be sure of it, Mr. President," Doc agreed. "Strange, isn't it, to wear such an indelible, identifiable mark, but go to the trouble of getting it done in secret?"

"But it does help them keep their numbers a mystery," the President said.

"In the process," Doc added, "they obscure the size of

the organization and the money needed to run it...which in turn protects the maniacal person or persons pulling the strings. Which brings me to my last and biggest question, Mr. President. One of the Guardians we arrested down here panicked and let slip something about the 'Keeper.' Has that shown up on the FBI's radar anywhere else? And does it ring alarm bells for you, like it does for me?"

"The Keeper?" the President asked quietly. "You're not thinking the guy was referring to Jonah Baird? That's the most outrageous thing I've ever heard!" the President roared. "I've known Jonah for decades. He was friends with my father, for Christ's sake. Just like your father was, Doc. He's a rock solid American through and through. I recall you telling me a while ago that he called himself the Keeper when he contracted you to find the lost treasure of the Knights Templar. But there's no way he's the 'Keeper' your suspect was talking about."

"Well then it's a hell of a coincidence," Doc said. "And coincidences always make me nervous. But the surest way to identify the Keeper is the same as always: follow the money. There's an awful lot of it being spent. And Jonah Baird has plenty."

"But not even *he* has enough to secretly run an operation this size," the President said.

"Which could explain the need to extort money with a nuclear device," Doc said. "Mr. President, after I get my crew settled in Montana again, I need to fly back into D.C."

"I'll arrange it right now and I look forward to your return," the President said. "When you're ready to come, call Chief Master Sergeant Samual Hollister. He'll know what to do. Be well, my good friend. In the meantime, take care and God bless!"

"Thank you, Mr. President," Doc said just before President Preston ended the call.

As Doc tucked his phone away, he realized the SUVs had arrived and airmen were helping his crew load their luggage. So he grabbed his suitcase and old Navy-issued duffle bag and headed down the broad porch steps. When he got home, he'd discover that Jim had slipped a CornerShot into the duffle bag as a going away present.

"I'll follow you in the second Suburban along with my crew," Doc told the master sergeant commanding the detail.

"Where are you all going so fast?" Jim boomed as he came out the front door with Anne.

"Don't worry, pop," Louis quickly answered. "We're not going anywhere without your famous bear hug and Mom's perfect hug."

"We miss you, and Jenny, and everyone else already," Anne said and teared up.

"We won't be gone too long, Mom," Jenny called to her. "I promise!"

"We're going to hold you to that, Marine!" Jim replied. "Thanks again folks, for taking good care of Sugar Tree while we were away. It already feels like we never left."

After handshakes, hugs, and kisses all around, the SUVs pulled onto Breckenridge Lane and were quickly gone.

"I am truly going to miss Jim and Anne and Sugar

Tree," Marsha sighed and pulled Q's arm tight around her shoulders.

"I can't do much about missing Jim and Anne, but I'll gladly build you a clone of Sugar Tree if you want one," Q told her sincerely.

"That's a wonderful idea!" Marsha shouted. "I would absolutely love that!"

"It would make visiting you two all the more fantastic," Louis told them.

"If you build it near our place, I'm sure the town will let you put in a long approach road and name it Breckenridge Lane. Then you could even give your Sugar Tree the same address."

"That's a tempting idea," Q said. "But I think I prefer to name the road Marshall Street."

"Your road, your choice," Doc conceded.

"Does this mean we're actually going to have you two as neighbors?" Connie asked.

"Uh huh!" Marsha answered excitedly. "Q and I have decided to retire."

"Well, kinda retire," Q emphasized.

"We were saving this as a surprise for later, but now I just have to share it," Madeleine said excitedly. "Noah and I want to build a place on the lake too!"

"Oh my heart's about to burst!" Connie shouted and hugged Doc. "I'm so very happy!"

"Don't be too happy," Doc said wryly. "You know we three guys don't get along well."

"Yeah, rrrright!" Madeleine shot back, sarcastically, and Connie and Marsha laughed.

Louis and Jenny sat quietly in the back row and were

a little puzzled by all the talk about building large homes in rural Montana with long access roads. They were dying to know how it would all be paid for, but thought better of asking, and opted to simply keep listening in the hope of figuring it all out in the days ahead.

Patience, Louis, patience, the marine silently reminded himself of Jenny's watchword.

Jenny silently reminded herself too, and their patience paid off. During the six-hour flight from Georgia to Washington State, Doc and the rest of the team told the long, adventurous story of how they met and embarked on a mission in Israel that eventually made them all wealthy enough to live comfortably in their "retirement." Of course, the whole story, including the part about the 700-year-old Templar Knight would have to wait until they all knew each other better.

"So now that we've finished that story," Doc said, "who would like to explain the President's remark that our lawn has been repaired?"

"Well, for one thing, a Homeland Security agent drove a huge SUV over it—twice—when the ground was muddy," Connie said.

"And then the helicopter landed on it—twice—when he came to evacuate us," Marsha said excitedly.

"Why did a Homeland Security agent drive across our lawn twice?" Doc asked.

"He was trying his best to rescue us, but personally I think Connie did a better job of it," Marsha explained.

"And what about the helicopter?" Doc asked.

"Same thing," Marsha said. "Except, Connie can't fly a helicopter."

"You got a point there," Doc agreed.

"I'm sure she'll explain it all to you in time," Marsha said.

"I hope so," Doc said, as he looked at Connie and sighed.

"It's really a very simple explanation, John," Connie said.

"I can't wait to hear the part about how you're always more careful than me," Doc told her.

"Well, we'll discuss it soon," Connie said.

"Soon?" Doc repeated as a question.

"Soon," Connie repeated as an assurance.

The six hours aboard the plane zoomed by with life stories and rapid-fire questions about past missions and mysteries still very much alive. Jenny and Louis had so much they wanted to know about each of their new friends as individuals and about "the team" they had all come together to form. Louis swapped fishing, hunting, and military stories with the other men, while Jenny sat almost silent as she listened tirelessly to the other wives talk about "the team."

"We must be boring you to death with our stories," Connie softly apologized to Jenny.

"Oh, no!" Jenny quickly answered. "There's so much I want to know about all of you, about your lives before you met and how you all came together to form the amazing team you are. How does a nurse in Washington, D.C., a special needs teacher in Maryland, and a paleographer in Rome meet the men you came to love and marry, then meet one another and become best friends? Even more incredible, you and your husbands comprise a team of adventurers for whom the President of the United States arranges spur-of-the-moment flights across the country aboard military aircraft—or like today, in his personal 757. No one Louis and I know, inside the Marine Corps or outside, excluding his parents of course, would believe a team like yours even exists, except in the imagination of some writer of action novels. Yet here you all are, and here I am with you! There's absolutely nothing boring about that!"

The stories, questions, and laughter helped compress the time, and the pilot announced they were approaching Fairchild Air Force Base much sooner than seemed possible. As soon as the plane landed, the team transferred to a luxurious Sikorsky S-92 executive helicopter, bound for Montana's Flathead Lake, two and a half hours away. That leg of the trip was Louis' chance to get some questions answered by the men of the team.

"I'm sure the details of how you all met and signed on for this life will come soon enough," he began. "But how did it happen that you do what you do? Where does the federal government's involvement end and your involvement begin...and why?"

"The simplest answer is that we met because we were meant to," Doc said. "Everything happens for a reason, Louis. Believing and remembering that will serve you well in making sense of the extraordinary challenges we encounter and the ways we overcome them."

"That part may be the easiest," Louis replied. "I've always believed everything happens for a reason."

"Perfect!" Doc replied. "Now, the more complicated answer is that President Preston is an excellent judge of character and a brilliant strategist and manager. He set the events in motion that brought us together and helped enable us to jell into the team we've become. And believe me, it's not lost on any of us that the President has added you and Jenny to the team. That fact alone supports what Q and Noah and I recognized soon after meeting the two of you. We're a better team with you among us...and we're happy to have you onboard."

"Thanks, Doc," Louis said quietly. "I'm grateful for the opportunity."

"And now that you're part of the team, you should know that our greatest value to the nation is plausible deniability," Doc explained. "We go where agents of our country are not authorized to tread. The lines we cross cannot be crossed...and we seek information and solutions that can only be had by crossing those lines. Our successes will never be known to the nation. But if and when we ever fail, we will be known as crackpot misfits on an imaginary mission with delusional motivations. We will shoulder the blame for the sake of the nation's reputation and honor."

"That's the heaviest job description I guess I will ever hear," Louis said as he sat upright.

"And for the record...you never heard it," Doc informed him. "And one more thing, Louis. There was no harm in it at Fairfield, but you and Jenny must get out of the habit of saluting military personnel we interact with. I know it will be difficult at first. But there must be no clue that we are United States representatives in any capacity—especially military. Those we cross paths with don't know who we are, and almost never have any idea of what our objectives are. You must have noticed that, for the most part, aircraft and motor vehicles we ride in lack the typical marks and insignias of the United States. The President must be able to keep us, and our activities, a secret. And so must we."

"Roger that, Doc!" Louis responded energetically. "I know," he then quickly said. "I'll work on dropping that response too."

"Perfect!" Doc replied.

When the Sikorsky's landing gear touched down on Doc and Connie's sprawling front lawn, the former Navy SEAL led the team out of the helicopter and up the broad front steps of his home. He'd only been gone a week but to him it seemed like a month.

"Home sweet home!" he shouted as he dropped his suitcase and duffle bag just a few steps inside the front door and marched around the huge living room.

"Oh my, you can say that again," Connie chimed in as she entered the house.

"Home sweet home!" Doc shouted even louder with his muscular arms spread wide.

It was the beginning of three blissfully unstructured, unaccountable days of rest, great conversations, wonderful home-cooked meals, luncheon barbecue cook-outs under a warm sun in the front yard overlooking magnificent Flathead Lake, and sharing dreams of what the team might do once the missions came to an end. Late in the evening of the third day, Doc gently rocked with his arm around Connie's shoulders on the front porch swing and the two of them took in the tranquil sight of dozens and dozens of boats anchored in the lake below with their cabins illuminated by soft lights as they rocked peacefully to the rhythm of the water.

"How is it that we ever leave this place, John?" Connie asked. "Are we sure we have our priorities in order and the things of the world in perspective?"

"Yes, I believe we do, Beauty," Doc sighed and seriously considered Connie's question. "I know it's tempting to think we've served our time, fulfilled our obligations, maybe even grown too old for the missions we accept. But the adrenalin still flows in the midst of our missions, and our successes still benefit the nation. We both know the day is nearing when we will pass the torch, and I admit that I look forward to it a bit more every day.

"But I know these Guardians of the Forbidden Library must be stopped or the nation, and perhaps the entire world, will be overrun by them."

Connie could tell by the tone of Doc's voice that another mission would soon take him away from her and their home. She just knew it.

"Do you have to go back to D.C. so soon, John?" she asked, fearing his answer.

"I'm afraid so, Beauty," he said. "I'll call and make the arrangements in the morning. But for now, I'm bushed and ready for a good night's sleep."

"I hoped you would say that," she cooed to him. "Come to bed and let me try to make you stay home forever."

"I trust your best efforts, Beauty," Doc chuckled in anticipation. "And I'll do my best to return the favor."

"I know you will, you handsome sailor," she said with a foxy smile. "I know you will."

14

HUNTING THE KEEPER

The next morning, Doc called Chief Master Sergeant Hollister to coordinate his D.C. trip.

"When will you make the trip, Doc?" the chief asked.

"The sooner the better, Chief," Doc answered. "I want to get in and get out ASAP."

"I can have a chopper to you by noon," the chief told him. "You'll be here at Fairchild by 1400 hours and I've got a two-seater F-100 Super Sabre that's been reassigned to Andrews. If you don't mind riding in the second seat for four hours, I can have it fueled and waiting for you. That'll get you into Langley at about 2000 hours, D.C. time, for a late supper. Good enough?"

"Perfect," Doc said, simply. "I'll be ready. Thanks, Chief."

"At your service, Doc," the chief replied. "The President said we're to have a car ready for you at Andrews too. The keys will be waiting for you."

"I can't thank you enough, Chief," Doc said sincerely.

"You can't thank me at all, Doc," the chief chuckled. "Taking good care of America's finest is my job. I won't be here when you arrive. So I'll wish you Godspeed now, Doc. Have a good flight and maybe I'll see you when you get back."

"I look forward to meeting you, Chief," Doc said. "Thanks again!"

Doc and the others heard the chopper approaching the house at noon exactly.

"Are you sure you have everything you'll need?" Connie asked him, as always.

"Everything but you, Beauty," was Doc's standard reply as he hugged and kissed her.

"Geeez!" Q said. "You're only going to be gone for a day or so, not a year."

"It'll feel like a year," Doc replied over his shoulder and kissed Connie once more.

"It will for me too," she whispered back to him.

"You sure you don't want me to go with you, Doc?" Q asked as Doc exited the house.

"Not this trip, Q," Doc answered. "I'll only be gone long enough to get answers to a few nagging questions for myself before we get any more involved in hunting down Guardians."

"That could take a mighty long time in D.C.," Q said, only half joking. "I see you're taking the cane I had made for you. Is your back bothering you again, or do you expect to use it for something other than walking?"

"I just need to have something with me to remind me of you, Q," Doc said facetiously. "I'm taking the Corner-Shot too."

"Go ahead and make a joke of it, Doc. But you know it's true," Q told him.

"That Q is a funny guy, isn't he?" Noah asked Louis at the far end of the porch, loud enough for everyone to hear it.

"Sounds like a lovers' quarrel to me," Louis said with a shrug of his shoulders.

"The two of you can be replaced, you know," Q told them with disdain.

"That might be to everyone's mutual benefit," Noah crowed back at him.

"Don't push that too hard, or we just might find out." Q played along out of boredom.

"You can't fire us, Q, and Doc knows our value," Noah said and shook with laughter.

"I'm out of here!" Doc shouted and broke into a run to the chopper.

"Bye, Baby!" Connie called out after him.

"Be back before ya know it!" he called back, and was quickly gone.

Strong tailwinds got Doc to Joint Base Andrews well before 8:00 p.m. He tossed his duffle bag and cane into the back seat of the big F-350 pickup that was waiting for him and headed to the studio apartment he still rented above the café on the north bank of the Potomac River, in the shadow of the Francis Scott Key Memorial Bridge. Doc kept it for just such a time as this. It was comfortable and out of the way—just what he needed to stay off the radar while in D.C.

Doc swung through a drive-thru and picked up a couple of burgers and an ice tea to fill the void in his stomach before calling it a night. He planned to turn in early because he wanted to get an early start in the morning. But even with a full stomach, he couldn't sleep. His mind wouldn't let go of the mystery he hoped to solve in the morning.

Doc tossed and turned for hours as he wrestled with the haunting question of whether Jonah Baird was the Keeper referred to by one of the Guardians apprehended in Georgia. Baird had originally introduced himself to Doc as the Keeper when he contracted Doc to find the lost treasure of the Knights Templar, nearly two years earlier.

Could it be just a big coincidence? Doc asked himself silently as he lay sleepless in bed and stared at the ceiling. The Keeper, whoever he was, had to be wealthy and very secretive, Doc reasoned. Baird was both. He had to be well-connected too. And Baird was as well-connected as anyone could be, from the Pentagon, to Congress, to the White House.

Doc often struggled with questions and coincidences in his line of work. So it was no wonder these kept him awake late into that first night back in his old apartment. He finally fell asleep sometime after 3:00 a.m., and of course, dreamed about the Keeper. In his dream, Baird was indeed the Keeper and had built an elaborate "Forbidden Library" in the basement of St. John's church, where Doc first met Baird two years before. Accessible only by a hidden door behind the alter, the library contained row after row of finely built mahogany shelves stocked with books and paintings and films and recordings he judged to be offensive. Their creators paid for their offenses with their lives. Doc dreamed that Baird fiendishly ordered the murders that were staged to look like suicides. Then he obsessively collected and displayed small souvenirs he thought would never be missed from each of the murders as grotesque trophies to commemorate the elimination of the offending creators.

In his dream, Doc ran across Lafayette Park to the White House to alert President Preston, but the north entrance doors were locked. Doc banged on the doors but no one came to open them. Then, as can only happen in dreams, the President suddenly placed a hand on his shoulder.

"What's wrong, Doc?" the dream President asked.

"It's Baird, Mr. President!" Doc shouted breathlessly. "Baird is the Keeper!"

"You're wrong, Doc," the dream President replied. "Baird's my friend."

"Come with me and I'll show you!" Doc shouted back at the dream President and led him across the park to St. John's Church. With only his pocket LED flashlight for illumination, Doc led the dream President behind the alter, through the hidden door, and down stone steps that wound their way to the dark, dank basement, which Baird had converted to his Forbidden Library. Doc threw open the library's ornate double oak doors...and found it completely empty, totally bare to the four ancient, musty brick walls laid in 1816.

Doc jolted awake from his dream at 4:30 a.m., surrendered to his sleeplessness, and moved from his bed to the worn, squeaky office chair beside it. The move instantly transported him back to the dark days and months following his medical retirements: first from the SEALs and then the Secret Service. In those days, his pain was so debilitating he could barely walk, and his uncertainty about the future was so severe he thought he'd never be happy again.

Doc slumped in the chair and surveyed the second-hand desk he bought back then for $40 at a resale shop so he could work on the ill-fated autobiography his late friend, Kenesaw Mountain Matua, had convinced him to write. He then recalled how putting his feet up on it brought some much-needed relief from the pain in his hip and back. Doc picked up his cell phone from the desk and relived the morning it rang and he first spoke to "Mr. Oliver," who ultimately led him to the Keeper, Jonah Baird.

Doc rocked back in his chair, put his feet on the desk, and stared out the tiny apartment's only window at the first light of morning. In that moment, he recalled how it felt to hear Baird's offer of a trip to Switzerland, where an experimental surgical procedure ended his pain forever. In return, Doc embarked on the quest that ended in Israel, where he, Q, Noah, and Madeleine found the lost treasure, which ended all of their concerns about money and the future.

The critical mass of good and bad memories spun themselves into a chain-reaction of emotions that made Doc's head and heart spin. The soldier of fortune owed his reclaimed vitality and high aspirations to Baird. If not for the wildly successful and secretive CEO, Doc would not only still literally be limping through life, he would have never married Connie or even met Q, Noah, and

Louis, or Marsha, Madeleine, and Jenny—all of whom had become indispensable parts of the rich, rewarding life he now enjoyed.

That's when Doc's most chilling memory of those days slammed into all the others. During their first meeting in a hidden corner of the basement of St. John's Church, within sight of the White House, Baird said something that now took on a whole new, diabolical meaning. Doc vividly recalled that as he considered Baird's offer of surgery and a bounty for finding the lost treasure, Baird told him he planned to use the proceeds "for the benefit of all mankind."

At the time, Doc thought Baird's plan was to use the money to develop groundbreaking, high-cost space exploration technologies. But now that Doc had helped uncover a hugely expensive international terrorism ring that was murdering writers, artists, and other creative types, he realized that Baird's words might have had an entirely different, terrifying meaning. So Doc's mission in the nation's capital was clear: He had to determine as quickly as possible whether or not Baird was the maniac the Guardians called the Keeper. And if so, he must apprehend him and bring his global reign of terror to an end.

When the morning had fully arrived, Doc slipped into the baggiest pair of cargo pants he owned, slid his 45 and two extra clips into his shoulder holster, then donned a bulky hoodie to cover it all so he could blend into the crowds of D.C. For good measure, Doc put the Corner-Shot into his backpack and slipped it on. As he headed out the door, he grabbed his cane, but then thought twice about taking it with him. Though he wanted to take it because he had for all his previous D.C. walks—and the SEAL Trident inlaid in its handle had gotten him into the basement of St. John's Church—he thought it might make him stand out, and that he did not want. So he popped the Trident free, stuck it in the right thigh pocket of his cargo pants and set off on what was once his daily trek. He walked east on Canal Road to Water Street, then up K Street to Pennsylvania Avenue. St. John's Church was just four blocks east on H Street, across from Lafayette Square, in clear sight of the White House.

A block before Doc reached the church, he paused in front of the Grange Building, home of Quest Publishing, where he had received the $20 gold piece that got him into the inner sanctum of the church on the fateful day he first met the Keeper. He smiled to himself when he recalled how a man who called himself "Mr. Oliver" lured him there with an offer to publish his autobiography, and then sent him away with the gold piece and instructions to give it to a priest who was waiting for him inside the church.

Doc's moves were more deliberate on this particular morning than they were on his first visit to St. John's. Though both visits to the "Church of the Presidents" were shrouded in mystery, the one set before him was a matter of life and death. So he approached it a lot more deliberately and considered each move before making it. Instead of rushing in as he did on his first visit, he casually walked along the sidewalk on 16th Street and took the time to talk with the hot dog vendor working the corner that morning.

"Good morning, sir!" the vendor said. "How would you like a hot and delicious, freshly prepared hot dog and perhaps an ice-cold beverage on this fine day?"

"It sounds too good to pass up, Marcus," Doc said, reading the name on the man's shirt.

"Call me Doc, and I'll take two with mustard and a sweet tea, if you have it," Doc said.

He thought it was awfully early for hot dogs, but he enjoyed the aroma just the same.

"Two with tea, comin' right up, Doc!" Marcus replied cheerfully.

"How's business this morning?" Doc asked to kick off the conversation.

"It's been slow, but it's early," Marcus said. "You're my first customer of the day and I got a feelin' that means things are about to pick up."

"Glad to hear it!" Doc said. "Do you work this corner every day, Marcus, or do you move around town?"

"Oh no," Marcus replied. "This here's *my corner*. I've worked this spot every day for the past three years."

"*Every day*?!" Doc asked in surprise.

"*Every day*!" Marcus replied emphatically. "It's a great spot and I don't intend to lose it."

"I'll bet you get a lot of foot traffic this close to the White House," Doc said.

"Yes, sir!" Marcus answered. "Especially on Sundays."

"Sundays?" Doc echoed with even more surprise. "Why's that?"

"St. John's is a very busy church," Marcus answered. "It's the Presidents' Church. Every President since James Madison has attended services here at one time or another. So the crowds can be huge and there are always visiting speakers and clergy coming and going."

"Have President Preston and the First Lady attended yet?" Doc asked.

"Many times," Marcus told him. "Whenever they're in town."

"Is the church open to the public this time of day?" Doc asked.

"Always!" Marcus answered.

"So I can just walk in and expect to get some quiet time?" Doc asked.

"Yes, sir," Marcus replied. "The priest don't usually show up 'til the afternoon."

The hot dogs were good, and Doc took time savoring them to digest what he'd just heard.

How ironic would it be, Doc silently asked himself, *if Jonah Baird was orchestrating an international terror organization right under the nose of the President of the United States? It seems too outrageously bizarre to be true. But it makes some sense,* Doc thought in the next moment. *Who would ever think to look here for clues to an organization that's killing people around the world?*

"Thanks for the great hot dogs and conversation, Marcus. Here's another president for you," Doc said as he handed the friendly vendor $50 and said, "Keep the change."

"Thank you, Doc!" Marcus said with a big, genuine smile. "I told you I had a feelin' things were about to pick up! Hope to see you again soon—hungry or not."

"I'll make a point of it next time I'm in town, Marcus,"

Doc replied and strode up the front steps of the church, hoping he would be alone inside.

He silently entered the church as though he were on a rescue mission. In one sense, he was. He vowed to rescue the truth from a truckload of his own conjecture and imagination. He was determined to put his worst fears to rest and leave the building with proof of whether or not Jonah Baird —the man he called the Keeper—was also the man the Guardians called the Keeper. And, like most every other mission Doc had ever embarked upon, he opened the door with next to no idea what he'd find on the other side.

"Here goes nothin'!" Doc told himself cautiously, and stepped through the door.

As Doc had hoped, the church was empty. He knew he couldn't count on it staying that way. So he ran up the center aisle and the three steps to the alter. He paused there and surveyed the sanctuary to ensure no one had followed him. Satisfied that he was alone, Doc ran behind the alter to the door he knew led to the room, where a pedestal stood the last time he was there. His heart raced as he grasped the doorknob.

It's open! he shouted in his head, and entered the room.

Strangely, the books that filled the shelves inside on his first visit were gone. The pedestal was still there and still held the book he needed in order to go any farther. Doc quickly opened the book's heavy cover and rifled through its pages in search of the cavity carved in the shape and size of his SEAL Trident somewhere within them.

Yes! Doc thought when he found it, then pulled the Trident from his pocket and pressed it into the cavity. Just as it had before, it opened a hidden door behind some shelves.

YES! he shouted in his head as he quickly returned the Trident to his pocket and stepped through the secret door he knew would close behind him momentarily.

Before Doc had time to think about it, he found himself back in the hidden room where he first met Jonah Baird and accepted the challenge of finding the lost Templar treasure. In that room were the two high-back chairs he and Baird sat in and struck their bargain. Doc would fly to Switzerland for the surgery that would end his crippling pain. After he recovered, he would search for the treasure that Baird said he would use "for the good of all mankind."

The thought of what Baird's words might have actually meant gave Doc chills and drove him to find the truth once and for all. He remembered that Baird silently and suddenly appeared behind him that day as he sat waiting for the meeting the mysterious CEO had arranged. So Doc walked to the wall directly behind the chair he'd once sat in and carefully ran the palms of his hands over every inch, searching for a trace of the door that must be there.

It took a few minutes, but Doc pressed more firmly on the wall and finally felt a section of it "give" slightly under the pressure. Certain he had found the hidden portal, Doc reached into another pocket of his cargo pants for the LED flashlight he'd used in his dream the night before. He shined the light along the wall at an angle, looking for a telltale ridge or seam he could pry to open the door he was sure he'd found. There was no stopping him now.

Found you! Doc thought when a ridge appeared under the harsh light.

No longer concerned about not leaving any trace of his having been there, Doc thrust the blade of his Schrade SC90 into the ridge. The razor-sharp knife easily sliced through the wallpaper that concealed the door and pried it open. Doc stood at the threshold for a moment. He was certain he was about to solve the most macabre mystery of his life. Whatever awaited him beyond that door would either prove that Baird was harmless and had innocently picked a wretched alias, or that he was, in fact, the Keeper, and had mercilessly orchestrated murders around the world for the past two months...and Doc had been his unwitting accomplice.

Determined to find the truth, the former SEAL descended the stairs just beyond the doorway, to a basement about the size of the one in his dream the night before. Doc located a light switch and flipped it on to reveal row after row of elaborate seven-foot-tall wooden bookcases. From where he stood, he clearly saw Culver Ainsley's last novel propped upright like a coveted trophy beneath a carefully aimed light. Beside it was what had to be the missing cap to the prescription bottle investigators found on Ainsley's nightstand the day he was murdered.

"What have I helped this madman do?" Doc asked in the room that Baird—the Keeper—had transformed from the foundation of the "Presidents' Church"...to the "Forbidden Library."

15

UNBROKEN ARROWS

D oc's heart raced inside his chest and his breathing was labored. Two bookcases held undeniable evidence of other authors, artists, rappers, and the like murdered thus far. The dozens of shelves that stood vacant and waiting for the grizzly "trophies" the Keeper still planned to collect bent Doc's mind and soul and screamed for him to bring the murder spree to an end!

The former Shadow warrior was overwhelmed by the reality that he'd been used by the Keeper for the most evil of purposes. Doc was no stranger to death. But he abhorred the killing of innocents. He'd dedicated his life to protecting the vulnerable—including the President— from the killers in their midst. Doc pulled out his cell phone and quickly photographed the items he saw in the library, and then remembered it was useless in the building on his last visit. No signal!

Doc knew he must tell the President and send the photos. To do that, he needed a signal. So he had to get out of the basement. That was when he heard the door open at the top of the stairs.

Damn it! Doc thought. *The die is cast!*

It could only be a Guardian or Baird coming down the stairs, which meant shots could be fired. So Doc turned out the light, took a position behind a bookcase, silently set his backpack on the floor, took out the CornerShot, inserted his 45 mm, and turned it on.

Come and get it! he thought to himself with his trigger finger ready and waiting.

"Come out with your hands up!" a voice rang out. "I won't shoot you if you come out. But I won't be so generous if I have to come down there and drag your lifeless body out!"

It wasn't the Keeper's voice. So Doc said nothing, gambling that his silence would ratchet up the intruder's anxiety. But Doc hadn't bargained on the tear gas canister that came tumbling down the stairs. As the canister reached the foot of the stairs, the gunman raked the stairwell with what sounded to Doc like an AK-47. The shooter was definitely playing for keeps.

But Doc refused to play. He quickly flipped the CornerShot's night vision camera on and ran to the wall at the bottom of the stairs. Doc wrapped the CornerShot around the corner, locked onto the gunman, and fired three perfectly placed shots that ensured there wouldn't be return fire. Doc's eyes quickly began to burn and swell shut as he slung the CornerShot over his shoulder and felt his way up the stairs. Halfway up, he kicked the body of the gunman he'd killed and dragged it the rest of the way up into the daylight washing into the church to see who it was.

A few anxious seconds later Doc's eyes stopped watering and he could open them just enough to see the "Guardian" tattoo on the inside of the dead man's left wrist. The former SEAL was certain he hadn't been followed to the church. So the Guardian must have already been there and doing a lousy job of guarding the library entrance. Doc listened intently for footsteps and hoped the Guardian hadn't radioed for backup before he became a corpse. But he had!

The next sound he heard was the front door of the church being forcefully swung open. Doc got just a glimpse of the three new Guardians before he dove under the nearest heavy, solid oak pew. The trio all carried AR-15s and were clearly there to kill him. He intended to prevent that from happening and was thankful that he'd brought two extra clips for his 45. He was also thankful that the first few rows of pews lacked kneeling rails, which allowed him to silently roll on the marble floor from one to another.

Doc knew the Guardians thought they had him outgunned. But the CornerShot in his hands tipped the advantage in his direction. He hated the idea of shooting inside the centuries-old church and feared innocent visitors might unwittingly walk into the crossfire. So he had to end the standoff quickly. Silently, he lifted the Corner-Shot like a periscope and surveyed the sanctuary wall to wall. It almost seemed unfair to Doc that the Guardians couldn't see him, and didn't know he could see them. As they walked toward him, he fired three perfectly aimed shots.

Doc stretched out on the seat of the pew he'd hidden behind and lowered the CornerShot for a view of the aisle floor, where he saw the three Guardians lying completely motionless. He took just a moment to send his photos. Then he heard the front door open slowly and adjusted the CornerShot to see a pair of feet cautiously step inside the church. It was another Guardian.

"James!" the Guardian yelled. "Scott? Omar? Where are you? Fellas? Are you alright?"

Doc knew he had to act fast before an innocent person wandered into the church. He aimed for the Guardian's shin and fired. The 45 mm Hornady Custom XTP bullet was traveling at 1,055 feet per second when it severed the Guardian's tibia, then buried itself in the wall behind the target. The Guardian and his AK-47 hit the floor before he felt any pain, then writhed in agony as Doc approached him cautiously, kicked his gun out of reach, and waited until the Guardian caught his breath and could hear what Doc asked him.

"Where's the Keeper?" Doc asked calmly.

"I don't know what you're talking about!" the Guardian grunted through clenched teeth.

"I could shoot your other leg if you'd like," Doc threatened. "Where's the Keeper?"

"Go fuck yourself!" the Guardian shouted at Doc. "Ahhhhhhhh!" he screamed when Doc laid his booted foot upon the Guardian's broken leg.

"Imagine how much it will hurt if I break the other

leg and step on both of them at the same time," Doc calmly threatened. "Where's the Keeper?"

"I ain't tellin' you shit!" the Guardian managed to say despite his pain.

"You're pretty tough," Doc told him and knocked him out with the butt of the CornerShot.

Doc bound the Guardian's wrists with zip ties he always carried for such emergencies, then dialed the "black ops" number the President had given him during his Secret Service days and clearly spoke "Three and One" plus the address into the phone, then hung up and dragged the living and dead Guardians into a small room at the rear of the sanctuary. He stacked the dead bodies and sat on them until a "cleaning crew" of six pulled onto the sidewalk at the church entrance and entered with a stretcher and three body bags. As they did their job, Doc quietly left.

"Hey, Doc! What'd ya think of the church?" Marcus asked as the former SEAL descended the front steps and walked toward H Street.

"Very, very interesting, Marcus," Doc replied with a wave. "Thanks for the info—and the dogs. See you next trip!"

Doc relaxed just a bit, knowing that by now his photos were in the FBI's hands.

"I'll be here, God willin'!" Marcus answered and waved back.

A long walk and careful thought in the park helped Doc realize that Guardians seemed to be everywhere the Keeper needed them. Equally interesting was the impression Doc got that the stairs he descended from inside the church may not have led to the building's basement, but simply to an underground chamber that merely "borrowed" the structure as a well-disguised entrance. Doc recalled that Marcus told him a priest was typically only available in the afternoon. But his first visit to the church was in the morning and a man dressed as a "priest" was waiting for him there. It was becoming clear to Doc that the Keeper specialized in illusion.

With that realization, Doc gained new perspective. He remembered how his first visit to the church two years earlier left him with questions that never got answered. What was the real identity of the man who called himself "Mr. Oliver"? How did he know Doc had begun writing an autobiography? Was the 1933 Saint-Gaudens Double Eagle gold piece he was given at Quest Publishing real? Was Quest Publishing real? Was the "priest" he gave the gold piece to real? Or were they all illusions? After all, in the Keeper's world, murders appeared to be suicides and the Forbidden Library appeared to be a church basement. Up was down and down was up.

Doc's second reason for wandering in the park was his concern that more Guardians might have been waiting for an "all clear" signal they never received, which could mean more of them were now on his trail. But that didn't appear to be the case, which provided another clue regarding the scale and sophistication of the Guardian force. Though there clearly were many of them, they seemed to operate more like a very large gang of henchmen than a para-military organization. That would explain why Doc and his team had such relatively easy success in confronting them. It also explained why the President opted to dispatch Doc's team instead of the FBI. With each new insight, Doc grew more certain the President new more than he revealed.

In those few mind-bending minutes Doc walked across Lafayette Square Park to Pennsylvania Avenue and stared at the White House from a park bench. His new perspective weighed on him and freed him at the same time. The insight he gained that morning raised questions about the missions of the past two years. But he now realized the answers didn't really matter. What mattered was he was finally able to see the big picture. The Keeper shrouded his maniacal plot in illusion, and President Preston was using the Keeper's own strategy in an effort to stop him. Doc now understood the role he and his team played in this deadly game of cat and mouse. The President had no idea who the Keeper would murder next. His only trump card was the Keeper's need to subsidize his global murder spree and the Forbidden Library that memorialized it. So Doc figured it was the President himself, and not a traitorous leaker, who

had the Keeper believing the United States would pay a high ransom for a lost nuclear device—a "broken arrow" in military parlance—to keep it out of terrorists' hands.

Doc now believed the President knew along that the Tybee Bomb was harmless. He'd simply used it to draw as many Guardians into the open as possible in the hope that one or more of them would rat on the Keeper in exchange for leniency. Doc also knew the U.S. has lost dozens of nuclear warheads since 1945—nine of them—where there was any hope of ever finding them. The

Tybee Island device was the best known, but Doc suspected the President had arranged for the Keeper to have the locations of all nine. And each time Guardians began sniffing around one of them, President Preston would unleash Doc and his team to catch them. Doc was angered by the thought that the President didn't trust him and his team enough to tell them the whole truth about the operation. He consoled himself with the belief that the President

acted in good faith and had to ensure the Keeper did not know the bombs were harmless.

As Doc rose from the bench, he knew he needed to meet with the President at least briefly before returning to Montana and embarking upon the next mission that would surely come. He knew the President was in town and the day was still young. So Doc thought his chances for a brief meeting were good. He entered the PIN on his Blackphone 2 and tapped the President's icon when it came on the screen. Doc knew his ID and location would instantly register on the President's end of the call and merely uttered "A-S-A-P" then hung up.

Once Doc made the call, the secure operating system let the President track him 24/7. The moment the President got Doc's voicemail, he knew precisely where Doc was in real time. The President then need only tap on the notification to dispatch a detail to deliver Doc to the White House and advise Doc it was on the way. With that base covered, Doc set off on the 45-minute walk to Arlington National Cemetery for the only other stop he'd planned for this trip: To pay his respects to his friend Kenesaw Mountain Matua. Doc made the visit whenever he was in D.C. But that day, he needed to thank his fellow SEAL for his friendship, loyalty, and sacrifice. At Mountain's funeral, Doc vowed to never forget what it meant to have known and fought beside him.

"I miss you, brother," Doc said quietly at the grave site, just 100 feet or so from the grave of Mountain's only genuine hero, President John F. Kennedy.

"Today, more than ever, I could sure use a talk with you, Mountain," Doc said. "You were the best of us, my brother. If not for your allegiance and valor, I would be buried here, being visited by you," Doc said, and was moved to recite the Warrior Team motto one more time. "True North is the compass deep within that guides me. It defines who I am as a warrior and as a human being. It is my fixed point in a spinning world. It anchors me. It is my value and honor as a person, my strength and worth to my team. No matter what decisions I must make, and actions I must take, True North tells me the way I must go. I'll be back soon, my brother."

Doc brought the visit to a close because he saw the familiar black SUV rolling slowly in his direction. It was time to lay all the cards on the table and talk turkey with the President. Once again, Doc was convinced everything happened for a reason. Had he not gone to St. John's Church that morning and been ambushed by Guardians it might have been quite some time before he figured out what was really going on. Now, he was headed to a briefing with President Preston with a new perspective that made him an equal partner in the hunt for the Keeper.

"Doc!" the President greeted him in his typically boisterous way. "Nice work! We got some very helpful information from the one who lived to talk about it...and I do mean talk."

"Hello, Mr President," Doc said flatly. "I'm happy to hear it. I hope what I have to say makes you as happy," he added, figuring the President hadn't yet seen his photos.

"Our meetings always cheer me, Doc. You know that," the President said with a smile.

"I do have important news for you," Doc began. "But I'm not sure you'll think it's *good news*. I found the Keeper's Forbidden Library right here in the capital, beneath St. John's Church this morning. I took photos of what I saw there. The best news is that although it appears construction is well along...it only contains the missing evidence from the murders we've suspected thus far. So we seem to be out in front of his massacre, and not merely following it. I'm sorry, Mr. President," Doc said solemnly. "But this means I was right. Jonah Baird is the Keeper who commands the Guardians of the Forbidden Library. He's insane and has to be stopped."

As Doc spoke, a stone-faced, well-dressed, impeccably groomed aide hurriedly entered the room and handed the President a leather-bound folder labeled *Top Secret*. The President moved to a far corner of the room and reviewed the contents. Doc thought it must be his photos.

"Follow me," the President said abruptly and led Doc down the main hall of the West Wing to the Oval Office. "Developments are unfolding fast on a number of fronts, Doc," the President said as he settled behind "Resolute," the big, carved mahogany desk that served several Presidents before him in times such as these...and worse.

Doc couldn't be sure if the "developments" the President referred to were related to the Keeper or other matters. He'd never know. What he did know in that moment was that he'd been shortsighted in thinking the President was merely being overly cautious in not sharing more about the Keeper and the Guardians. Doc now graphically understood that the President's plate was not only always full...but it often spins, sometimes nearly out of control. Those few moments in the presence of the Commander-in-Chief during just one interruption in a day full of them gave Doc a closeup look at the near-impossible challenge of leading the nation's 300 million souls through the countless perils of a world that seemed to always be on the brink of one disaster after another.

The glimpse Doc got that day of the burden carried by the President of the United States, leader of the free world, was so powerful it instantly matured his perspective in ways that left him with just one response when the President asked him to not stop until the Keeper was stopped.

"Yes sir, Mr. President," he simply answered.

"We've shut down the Keeper's Forbidden Library, Doc," the President said with only a slight grin. "But as you might predict, he's vanished. We're in the process of freezing his known assets and he's been added to the national No Fly list. But we both know he could be out of the country already. So we've issued an international alert for his arrest and return, just in case. If he's not stopped soon, he'll likely construct another Forbidden Library beyond our borders and resume his murder spree. Bringing him to justice will not be easy. Frankly, his 'terrorist' status will likely win him alliances that further complicate tracking him down. So our efforts must be silent and swift. The nation needs your best efforts more than ever, Doc!

"I'll make sure you have whatever you need," the President said. "Just let me know."

"Our only wild card is to quickly round up as many Guardians as we can, Mr. President," Doc answered. "With the Keeper's assets locked down, I believe the best way to do that is to bait the trap with what they believe will bring them the fastest cash. I figure you did that with the Tybee Bomb. Am I right?"

"That's correct, Doc," the President conceded. "I hope you understand that I needed to ensure there were no leaks regarding what we were up to. But I see now that cat's out of the bag."

"Best I know, the next most tempting Broken Arrow story is the one about how we lost a Mark 4 bomb on Kologet Mountain in British Columbia back in 1950. The story I've heard is that it's the same size as the "Fat Man" bomb we dropped on Nagasaki, Japan in 1945."

"We're just a little ahead of you, Doc," the President said with a grin. "We dangled it a week ago and just recently learned they've taken the bait. Our best guess is there are approximately a dozen Guardians trekking around the mountain right now. How soon can you have your crew ready to go?"

"Get the aircraft you think we'll need ready and I'll have my guys where they need to be in short order," Doc answered. "One more thing, Mr. President. We're going to need PHAZRs for this mission. I think you remember that we used them quite effectively when we evacuated Baird's brother from the *USS Ronald Reagan* two years ago. Give me a half dozen of them to carry with us and have one mounted to the belly of the chopper that delivers us to the mountain. I'll bring you every Guardian we find waiting for us out there."

"Consider it done," the President said abruptly. "I'll have a team take you back to where you're staying. How soon can you be ready to leave?"

"I'm ready now, Mr. President," Doc answered. "Get me to Andrews and I'll climb into whatever they think will get me back to Fairchild the quickest. My team will rendezvous with me there for the trip to the mountain."

"That's a lot of ground to cover and air to fly through, Doc," the President. "I don't see how you can do it so quickly and so well on such short notice. I'll make sure you have meals, blankets, and pillows on the flights."

"Well then we're even, Mr. President," Doc said with a grin.

"How so?" the President asked with a quizzical look.

"I don't see how on earth you can do your job as well and as quickly as you do with little or no notice. I commend you, Mr. President," Doc said, then shook the President's hand and left.

16

THE HIDDEN PLACE

Five hours later, Doc was singing in the shower to wake himself up at Fairchild Air Force Base, while Q, Louis, and Noah stretched out on the furniture just outside the locker room and hoped he would hurry up.

"Does he know he can't sing?" Louis asked with a laugh.

"He'll argue with you if you tell him that," Q replied.

"Whether he can sing or not, it's just wrong for a former SEAL to sign *Beauty and the Beast* in the shower," Noah laughed and shook his head.

Ten minutes later, Doc finished and emerged ready to go.

"I didn't know you guys were sitting right out here," Doc said.

"Would it have kept you from singing?" Q asked sarcastically.

"I would have picked another song," Doc answered.

"Would it have sounded better?" Louis asked.

"I gave it the best I got," Doc said with a shrug.

"That's tragic!" Noah said.

"Do you guys pick on each other when I'm not around?" Doc asked sarcastically.

"Not really," Q answered. "We still pretty much focus on criticizing *you*."

"That warms my heart, Q. It truly does," Doc told him with a chuckle. "Let's get supper and some sleep. I can brief you while we eat."

Supper was spaghetti and jogged Q's mind about the mission ahead.

"When's the next can of worms supposed to arrive?" he asked Doc.

"No worms this time around, Q," Doc replied. "Our mission is simple. Get in, knock 'em all out and bring 'em all back for interrogation. Hopefully, at least one of them knows the Keeper's location and we can bring this dumpster fire delusion to an end once and for all."

"What time we leavin' in the morning?" Noah asked.

"We'll board a CH-47 chopper at 0500 hours tomorrow and rendezvous with the carrier *Harry S. Truman* off the coast. The chopper will go with us, 300 miles up the coast of British Columbia overnight. Then we'll board the chopper again before dawn and head about 40 miles inland, where the Convair B-36 'Peacemaker' bomber crashed in 1950 while transporting the first nuclear device ever lost by the U.S. The real story, according to the Department of Defense, is that the crew dropped the bomb in the ocean before it entered Canadian air space and crashed near Kologet Mountain. But the Guardians believe the bomb was still aboard the plane when it crashed. So we'll find them near the crash site.

"We have the Defense Department coordinates that were leaked to the Guardians. So we'll do one high-level flyover to ensure we have a fix on their camp. The chopper will set down about a mile away and we'll hoof it to just outside the camp. Then the fun begins. The chopper will swoop in and zap 'em with the PHASR. In case the chopper's PHASR doesn't zap all of 'em, we'll each be carrying one. Q and I will carry two for backups. The weapon will give us approximately twenty minutes to handcuff 'em before they come to their senses, regain their sight, and we march 'em into the chopper for the flight back to the *Truman*. Our mission will be accomplished and interrogations will begin immediately onboard the carrier. Any questions?"

"Just one, but it's a doozy," Q said. "What the heck is a PHASR?"

"I'm glad you asked," Doc said with a grin. "A personnel halting and stimulation response rifle is the most humane weapon ever invented, gentlemen. It's the funniest looking rifle ever created. Six of them are waiting for us onboard the *Truman* and you'll know them when you see them. We will wear high-altitude flight suits and locking helmets with blacked out visors to shield our eyes from the PHASR rays. And no, you don't get to pilot a fighter on this mission."

"But what you are saying is that we won't use our side arms this trip?" Q asked.

"That's the plan," Doc confirmed. "The PHASRs will completely disorient and blind the Guardians for approximately twenty minutes. In fact, it will totally knock out most, if not all, of them. So side arms should be unnecessary. The government needs every piece of information about the Keeper and his whereabouts that the Navy interrogators can extract from the Guardians. So our mission from here on out is to round up as many of them as we can. Sooner or later, a Guardian is going to sing like a songbird."

"How do these PHASRs work?" Louis asked.

"Don't know," Doc answered. "I know you just have to point them like a shotgun, not aim them like a rifle. My SEAL team used them very effectively a couple of years ago." Doc smiled at the irony.

"What's so funny?" Q had to know.

"Remember when we first met?" Doc asked. "When you illegally entered my room without my consent at Walter Reed while I was trying to sleep after life-threatening surgery?"

"You wimp!" Q interrupted Doc's story, which Noah and Louis desperately wanted to hear. "It was a routine procedure to clean up a condition you were trying to milk for time off. And I was there on the authority of the President of the United States, not because I didn't have twenty other things I would have preferred to be doing."

"You really should be some politician's campaign advisor, Q," Doc said jokingly. "Anyway, the part you don't know—and can't lie about—is that my SEAL team used PHASRs on a mission that ultimately landed me in the hospital."

"Oh, *that's* comforting!" Q said with obvious misgivings about using the weapon.

"Don't worry," Doc assured him. "That was just a lack of experience on my part. I know how to use the technology now. Anyway, that mission evacuated Captain Augustus Baird—the Keeper's brother—from the *USS Ronald Reagan*."

"Really?!" Q sat up straight and asked in amazement. "You rescued Jonah Baird's brother?! And it's come to this?!"

"I wouldn't call it a rescue, exactly," Doc said cryptically. "But that's about all I can say about the mission, fellas. Sorry. But believe me, when you don't want casualties, PHASRs are the weapon to use. There will be time to learn how to use it onboard the *Truman* tomorrow."

"You must have some amazing stories that can never be told," Louis said to Doc as they left the mess and headed to bed for a night's sleep.

"A few perhaps," Doc said. "But just a few."

"I could make one up," Q teased Louis, "if you really think you need to hear one before going to sleep."

"You really are annoying," Louis told him. "Do you work at it, or does it just happen?"

"Do your best to ignore him," Doc told Louis, only half-kidding. "He gets this way when he's scared about a mission."

"I'm not scared," Q said defensively as he pulled his Stetson down over his eyes and reclined on his bunk with his black full-quill ostrich western boots still on.

"Those are mighty fancy boots for a soldier of fortune," Noah teased Q.

"All men should have my good taste in clothes and accessories," Q snidely replied.

"I saw The Village People in concert once and one of 'em had boots just like these," Noah poked at Q a little more.

"I rest my case," Q said, hoping to end the conversation.

"Would you both give it a rest so we can all get some sleep before 0500?" Doc pleaded.

Q pulled his boots off, stripped out of his jeans and shirt, and was first to fall asleep.

Doc awoke at 3:00 a.m., restless and thinking about the mission ahead. He wondered how many Guardians awaited his team and if they were well-armed. He hadn't exaggerated his confidence in the PHASRs they'd carry with them on the mountain. But he was well-acquainted with the unpredictability of battle. He recalled words of wisdom about warfare of the late President Dwight D. Eisenhower.

"Plans are worthless," the former World War II Supreme Allied Commander liked to say. "But planning is everything."

Eisenhower explained, "There is a very great distinction because when you are planning for an emergency ... the very definition of 'emergency' is that it is unexpected, and is not going to happen the way you are planning."

Doc's personal version was, "Plan and be ready for the unexpected."

Thinking as deeply as he could that early in the morning, Doc imagined the two worst things he thought could happen: First, like a sailor managed to do that fateful morning aboard the *Ronald Reagan*, a Guardian could be beyond the reach of the PHASR's ray and get the drop on one or more members of the team. And second, more than one Guardian would somehow be beyond the reach of the rays, hole up somewhere, and Doc and his team would have to figure out a way to get their captives to the chopper, while also managing a siege that could last for days, and require one of the nation's most powerful combat ships to anchor off the Canadian coast until all of the Guardians were aboard. Doc saw his challenge as avoiding both scenarios, but being prepared if one should unfold. So Doc planned to have his team pack extra rations and water.

The light mood of the evening before was history by 4:00 a.m., when Doc awoke his team and they quietly dressed, ate, and climbed aboard the CH-47F Chinook for the two-hour flight to the "Lone Warrior," the 1,100-foot-long nuclear-powered aircraft carrier *USS Harry S. Truman* and its 6,000-person crew of seamen and pilots awaiting them in the Salish Sea, less than a mile off Washington State's Olympic Peninsula, just south of Vancouver Island.

The only words uttered by the chopper pilot were his announcement that they were just ten minutes out from the *Truman*. Onboard the carrier, Doc, Q, and Noah were accustomed to the silent treatment they received from the crew. But Doc had to explain to Louis that, officially, the team was not onboard. Their mission was unknown to all but their Chinook pilot, who would airlift the Guardians to the *Truman,* and the four interrogators that were flown in the day before Doc's team to set up interrogation rooms near the carrier's brig and extract as much information as they could from the Guardians.

The secrecy gave Doc plenty of time alone with his team to review the plan and acquaint them with the PHASRs they'd carry into the Canadian wilderness. Meanwhile, the *Truman* navigated the Inside Passage to within five miles of Ketchikan, Alaska, their jumping-off point for the chopper flight inland to the crash site in the Canadian Rocky Mountains, nearly fifty miles east of Stewart, British Columbia, the region the indigenous population called the "Hidden Place." Doc also used the time to make sure his team understood that both the U.S. and Canadian governments would deny any knowledge of their presence or mission. They had to succeed, or they would be disavowed, charged, and tried as an "extremist radical group," and would likely be imprisoned for a minimum of three years.

After giving them time to handle the PHASRs, Doc had them suit up twice in the high-altitude flight suits and full-visor helmets. He didn't want any unexpected complications when they had to slip into the snug-fitting suits and lock the helmets on at 0400 hours the next morning.

The practice paid off and the morning went without a hitch as the team readied themselves and carried their PHASRs aboard the chopper and it lifted off from the *Truman* at exactly 0500 hours. Doc and the others zipped into their hooded parkas soon after takeoff. He wanted to be prepared in case the chopper went down in the mountains.

"Don't you think these are a little warm to be wearin' right now, Doc?" Q grumbled.

"It might be summer, but nighttime temperatures

here can reach -10 degrees," Doc told him. "I'd rather hear you moan about the parka now, than if we get stuck and have to stay warm until the sun comes up and we're rescued 3,000 feet above sea level."

"Point made," Q answered meekly.

But there were no hitches. The Chinook set down a mile out from the Guardian camp while twenty-three of the twenty-four who were there were still asleep. Louis used his PHASR to take out the one who stood watch, cuffed him, and stayed with him while Doc and the others roused the twenty-three who were sleeping. Fortunately, they were all in sleeping bags inside a large tent. So Doc simply ordered them all to look his way and Q and Noah zapped them with their PHASRs. Thirty minutes later, far sooner than Doc could have ever predicted, all two dozen Guardians were cuffed and sitting shoulder to shoulder on the floor of the chopper as it made its way back to the *Truman*. The interrogators had arranged for each of the captives to eat breakfast just prior to questioning.

Meanwhile, Q, Louis, and Noah enjoyed steak, eggs, potatoes, coffee, and juice, and returned to the berths for a well-deserved nap. Doc instead walked the deck of the *Truman* and took in the early morning beauty of the Inside Passage as the carrier made its way back out to the Pacific and the Olympic Peninsula. He was tired, but he needed time to process the quick success of the mission. The team had pulled it off flawlessly and Doc hoped it would result in the President learning where to find the Keeper.

Doc wasn't ready to say so to anyone, but he had

grown weary of this insane game of hide and seek. Though this foray went as smooth as silk, he knew that if they didn't bring the madness to an end soon it could get very ugly. People had been murdered because they had inadvertently offended the mind of a madman they'd never met. And more would suffer the same fate as long as the Keeper was able to command it and add their labors of love to the Forbidden Library, which he would no doubt rebuild somewhere else in the world.

As Doc stood at the rail near the *Truman's* bow and looked east in the direction of Montana, he longed for Connie and their home. He knew the men who stood and fought beside him felt the same longing for their wives and homes. He was grateful for them, and even more grateful that they shared his commitment to see this mission through, to find the Keeper, and deliver him to justice so the world would be a saner, safer place. Doc glanced at his cell phone to check the time. Fittingly, it was exactly high noon. Now all Doc needed was a call from the President telling him where to find the Keeper so he could call Connie and tell her when she might be able to expect him home.

17

"50 YEARS OF VICTORY"

D oc got the call he'd hoped for that evening after supper. He was attempting to defuse another poking session between Q and Noah when there came a sharp knock on the door of their compartment.

"Captain has an important call for your spokesperson up on the bridge," the sailor said.

"That would be me," Doc replied, and fell into step as the sailor hustled back to the bridge.

When Doc entered the bridge, the captain pointed to a booth in the far corner with a tiny LED light blinking over its door. Fascinated, Doc stepped into what looked every bit like a 21st century version of a pay phone booth of the 1940s. He stepped inside it and the door slid tightly closed behind him. He knew instantly it was completely soundproof. So he picked up the receiver and put it to his ear.

"This is Doc," he said simply.

"I know, I can see ya big fella!" the President's voice boomed on the other end.

Doc instinctively looked around for a camera, but didn't see one.

"Congratulations on another perfect mission, Doc," the President said. "Several of our songbirds are singing like you wouldn't believe. They've given us a truckload of new information about how the Keeper has shifted his focus to Russia and may even be there now. Doc, this comes at the perfect time! Our intelligence alerted me this morning that Russia's only Nobel Prize-winning poet, Sergei Romanoff, was found dead by a housekeeper when she reported to work.

"I just got off the phone with the Russian President and he went off like a Russian nuclear warhead when I advised him of the likelihood that he has a murder on his hands. He'd been assured it was an unfortunate case of alcohol poisoning and was busy planning a national memorial ceremony. Now the KGB will get their hooks into it and he'll have to sort through the propaganda to find out what really happened."

"You and I both know what happened," Doc said calmly. "It's all very unfortunate, but at least we have confirmation that the song our birds are singing is correct."

"Yeah, while I was on the phone with the President he confided that he had his own suspicions. Turns out a $9,000 bottle of Ladoga Group Russian Vodka the President gave him when the Nobel Prize was awarded wasn't in the liquor stash in the Moscow apartment where

Romanoff was found looking cozy in his expensive Russian hand-carved, four-poster bed."

"But one dead Russian poet doesn't prove the Keeper's there," Doc countered.

"Agreed," President Preston said. "But it's consistent with the scenario laid out by a couple of the Guardians you brought to the *Truman.* They told us the Keeper's in Russia on business. And our State Department was advised last month that Jonah Baird was headed to northern Russia on a business trip for his multi-billion dollar aerospace venture, Dark Yonder. But he's been incommunicado since he arrived in Moscow. The Guardians told us he plans to rebuild the Forbidden Library in an abandoned Doomsday Vault he purchased from the Russians on Big Diomede Island, smack in the middle of the Bering Strait."

"What the heck is a Doomsday Vault?" Doc asked, thinking he could guess the answer.

"It's not as ominous as it sounds, Doc," the President chuckled. "It's a safe place where countries store seeds in case they have a catastrophic crop failure or some other disaster that destroys vegetation on a major scale. The Russians built it during the Cold War and now have several more advanced vaults throughout their country. So do we, frankly."

"But what's it doing in the middle of the Bering Strait?" Doc asked. "Isn't that international water?"

"The Russians don't appear to think so," the President said matter-of-factly. "But that's an issue for another day. Right now, we have to capture the Keeper and bring an end to all this. I'll get the Russian President back on the phone after this call to negotiate putting your team on a Russian vessel. He'll put up a stink. Let Louis know I'm assuring the Russian President you're all civilians who have chased the Keeper for weeks. It's the only way I can get him to agree to work with us, because he knows so little about the Keeper and his Guardians and he can't afford to have this blow up in his face and have to explain more dead famous Russians.

"Bring the Keeper back to the U.S., Doc," the President said firmly. "If the Russian justice system gets ahold of him we'll never see him again...and neither will anyone else. This is an international matter and we don't need the Russians trampling all over every other nation's interests in bringing Baird and his henchmen to justice."

"Understood, Mr. President," Doc said simply.

"We'll fly your crew and gear to Eielson Air Force Base for a briefing," the President told him. "If you need something more, you can get it there. Good luck, Doc. Put a stop to this madness once and for all and I will be eternally grateful," the President said, and ended the call.

Doc, Q, Noah, and Louis used the encrypted phone booth to advise their wives they'd be gone one more week.

"I don't like this one bit, John!" Connie said in anger. "This mission is yanking you around the globe like never before and God only knows how dangerous it all is. In the meantime, I guess I'm supposed to bake cookies and keep the home fires burning."

"I know and I agree, Beauty," Doc said gently. "But we're so close to catching the Keeper and bringing an end to his killing. I wish I could tell you more, but I can't. I love you and I promise to make this up to you somehow when I come home. I also promise we'll talk about the future too. Okay? And please remember," Doc said, "everything happens for a reason."

"Okay," Connie said softly. "I love you, John. Come home as soon as you can."

Q, Louis, and Noah each had pretty much the same conversation with their wives. Then the four of them gathered their gear, reported to the flight deck, and were flown to Eielson Air Force Base in time for supper. While they attempted small talk during supper in a small, barren conference room, a stone-faced airman knocked on the door, then abruptly strode in, set a large can in the middle of their table, and left without a word. The four of them stopped eating and briefly stared at the can. Its handwritten label said *Worms*.

"I almost wish that was dessert," Q sighed.

"But you know it's not," Doc said with a hand on Q's shoulder, and presented the Schrade S90 to him, handle first, and asked, "Do you want to do the honors, or shall I?"

"You better do it," Q said warily. "I might use it on myself."

"Cheer up!" Doc said as positively as he could. "This can't go on much longer."

"I hear that's what Moses said," Q replied sarcastically.

Doc sliced the lid off the can and pulled out the briefing documents.

"Get your rest tonight, fellas," Doc said as he read the briefing papers. "We'll leave here at 0500 hours tomorrow aboard another Chinook CH-47F bound for Savoonga, a town on the northern tip of St. Lawrence Island so small you'll never hear of it again. A fishing boat will be waiting there to take us twenty miles out, due northwest, where we will board the Russian nuclear ice breaker *50 Years of Victory*."

"WHAT?!" Louis, Q, and Noah all shouted at once.

"We're going to board a Rooskie ship?" Q asked in disbelief.

"Calm down, fellas," Doc said firmly. "You've known all along this has been an international effort."

"Scotland Yard and INTERPOL sure," Q said. "But now it's the KGB too?!"

"Guardians murdered a famous Russian poet," Doc said. "The President wants to ensure the Keeper and his Guardians are tried in the U.S. and/or European courts before the Russians have their way with them."

"I say we should let the Rooskies have their way with the whole lot of them and save our country and all the others a lot of time and a pile of money," Q grunted. "Whatever the Rooskies do to the Keeper, he's earned it—and more."

"Do you feel better now, Q?" Doc asked sarcastically.

"I do! Thanks for letting me vent, Doc!" Q said with a smile.

"Are you finished?" Doc asked, just as sarcastically.

"I believe so, yes," Q said, still smiling.

"The Russian ship will take us to the north shore of Big Diomede Island," Doc said. "Here's a satellite photo of the concrete bunker doors to the Doomsday Vault."

"What do we know about those doors?" Louis asked.

"Not much—except they open several times a day," Doc answered.

"What for, and for how long?" Noah added his questions.

"Can't be sure, but it appears to be for cigarette breaks," Doc said with a shrug.

"You're kidding, right?" Q asked in surprise.

"Think about it, Q," Doc replied. "The island's uninhabited and as remote a location as you can find outside the Arctic Circle. They've just underestimated our ability to find them and quickly became complacent. That's all the better for us, right?" Doc asked rhetorically.

"Right," his three teammates said together, and were a bit more relaxed.

"We'll come ashore about a mile east of the vault, and then park ourselves out of sight outside the vault until the doors open," Doc said. "One of the Guardians singing back in D.C. was in the vault last week. So we have an inkling of its interior. Thankfully, we know where the control panel for the doors is located and how it works. Each of us needs to study this schematic because there's no telling which of us will be the one to open the doors—assuming they're closed when we are ready to leave."

"Forgive me, Doc," Q said cynically, "but this is the worst-laid plan I've ever seen!"

"I couldn't agree more, Q," Doc replied. "But it's a little better than no plan."

"Roger that!" Louis chimed in.

"I think the biggest catch is we that it's unclear how we'll get back to the ice breaker with the Keeper and however many Guardians we find there with him."

"Man, oh man, I don't like the feel of this, Doc," Noah said softly. "There are just so many unknowns. Like for instance, do we know if the Guardians are heavily armed?"

"We don't," Doc answered. "So we must assume they are and hope we're wrong. We'll carry our PHASRs at the ready because the President wants us to bring them all back alive. But we'll each also have a side arm and an XRail shotgun because I want to bring *all of us* back alive. And the XRails won't be loaded with rock salt this time, Noah."

"Thanks! That's comforting to know, Doc," Noah replied.

"On that note, gentlemen, I'm headed to my berth," Doc said. "See you back here at 0430 sharp for our trip to meet the Commodore of the *50 Years of Victory*. Goodnight!"

"Goodnight, Doc!" they barked together, and headed to their berths as well.

The team members didn't sleep well and converged back in the conference room earlier than planned the next morning. They climbed onto the CH-47F before 0500. As always, the pilot was silent until his ten-minute warning that they were approaching the Savoonga air field.

As they approached the coastal town, the team caught a glimpse of the *50 Years of Victory* awaiting their arrival less than a mile off shore.

"There she is fellas," Doc said, "approximately 100 *feet* wide and 400 feet long. She displaces approximately 25,000 tons and cuts through ice up to ten feet thick thanks to 75,000 horsepower generated by two nuclear reactors. She's an engineering marvel even we haven't matched. She's a sight to behold, ain't she?"

"And crawlin' with Rooskies!" Q just had to say. "But what's she towing?"

"Looks like a Russian version of our LACK," Louis excitedly told him.

"What's it do?" Noah asked.

"I believe it's our ticket to Big Diomede Island," Doc guessed out loud.

"You are correct," Louis said. "I've wanted to ride in one since I first saw a video during basic training. Just wait 'til you see what it can do!"

Doc quietly took in the sight of the LCAC and Louis' excitement and Q could see the wheels in Doc's brain spinning extra fast.

"What are you thinkin', Doc?" Q had to ask.

"It's too soon to know, Q," Doc answered. "But I *am* thinking. Stay tuned."

Fifteen minutes later, the team was aboard a nondescript fishing boat headed to a rendezvous with the Russian ice breaker. Doc and Louis were surprised they had to board the huge vessel via rope ladders. But they handled it well. Then they got a good laugh watching Q and Noah struggle, twist, and turn to complete the climb.

"What's so funny?" Q demanded to know.

"That was quite a sight!" Doc laughed. "Sure am glad you made it!"

Doc was pleasantly surprised that the six serious sailors who created them escorted all four team members to the bridge. He wanted to gain the confidence of the

Commodore and it looked like he might have a head start.

"Welcome aboard, Yanks!" the Commodore greeted them very loudly from across the bridge as they stepped in the door. "How do you do?"

"We aren't 'Yanks'! We're Americans!" Q barked back.

"Easy, Q," Doc said softly. "He's just trying to be friendly."

"It's a bad try!" Q barked back.

"I went to New York once eight years ago and met some Americans," the Commodore said loudly. "They were very nice!"

"We're pleased to meet you and your crew, Commodore Tarkoff," Doc said, and extended his hand. "Thank you very much for granting us passage aboard such an impressive vessel."

"*Fifty Years of Victory* is the pride of the Russian navy," the Commodore told them. "And I am very proud to be the Commodore. Make yourselves at home, gentlemen. Get comfortable. Eat if you are hungry. Just tell my crewmen and they will escort you to the mess. I hope you like Russian food."

I don't like anything Russian, Q somehow managed to only think and not say.

"At seventeen knots, we should reach Big Diomede Island at approximately 1800 hours. Senior Lieutenant Ivanov will take you ashore in the hover landing craft. When you get back, you must tell me what you think of it."

I don't like anything Russian, Q managed to only think again.

"Thank you very much, Commodore Tarkoff," Doc replied, and led his team off the bridge for a short tour of the ship's deck under the watchful eyes of dozens of armed, suspicious Russian sailors.

Doc and his teammates toured the ship for an hour before Louis tugged on Doc's sleeve.

"I'm starvin', Doc," he said, "and I'm wondering if that wonderful smell might be genuine Russian beef stroganoff."

"Let's find out," Doc said, and their guide led them to the mess.

To Louis' great pleasure, the mess was indeed serving beef stroganoff, as well as blinis and borscht. Louis had to try all of them. Noah and Doc did too. Q had a glass of orange juice.

"You don't know what you're missing, Q!" Louis gushed with his mouth full.

"And you don't know what they put in that stuff when they saw you coming," Q replied.

Doc and Noah just laughed and kept eating. They'd almost finished when Senior Lieutenant Ivanov strode to their table and introduced himself in perfect English.

"I'm pleased and proud to have been selected to pilot your landing craft this afternoon," he told them. "Would you like to see it now to get oriented to its safety features?"

"Absolutely!" Doc said, and quickly rose from the table along with his crew.

"It is a magnificent machine," Lieutenant Ivanov boasted as crewmen brought the landing craft near to the stern of the ice breaker, and he showed them how to jump aboard. "It's far superior to anything other nations have."

You sack of sea waste! Q managed to only think. *You stole the design and technology from us and the British!*

"You may be right," was all Doc said.

"This landing craft is approximately 50 feet wide and 90 feet long," Lieutenant Ivanov continued to boast. "She weighs roughly 100 tons and can carry up to 75 tons or 159 crewmen and all their equipment and support vehicles at least 200 miles at roughly 40 knots over land and sea, thanks to her four 1,000 horsepower turbine engines."

"Is it difficult to drive?" Doc asked innocently.

"Very—until you get the hang of it, which takes about eight weeks of training," Lieutenant Ivanov said earnestly.

I'll bet American seamen could drive this buggy just fine in one afternoon of training, Q managed to only think.

"Do you think I might be able to be able to take the controls for a few minutes when we're out at sea?" Doc asked.

"Perhaps," Lieutenant Ivanov said, "depending on sea conditions when we're out there."

"Thanks!" Doc said. "Could I just stand at the controls for a moment now?"

"I guess so," Lieutenant Ivanov replied naively.

Doc slid into the high-back operator's chair and gripped the wheel and throttle. There were four peddles at his feet. But he thought it best to wait until they were at sea to ask any more operational questions.

"Wow!" Doc gushed. "*This is an amazing machine!*"

"I think so, and I knew you would agree," Lieutenant Ivanov boasted.

"Damn, Doc!" Q barked when they were back aboard the ice breaker and Lieutenant Ivanov left them. "You were like a teenager with a '64 fastback Mustang. Get a grip!"

"That's our ticket out of here, Q!" Doc whispered excitedly. "It'll easily carry however many Guardians we capture and this tub will never catch us at 40 knots. The coastal town of Wales is only about fifteen miles east of Big Diomede Island and Commodore Tarkoff wouldn't dare chase us through U.S. waters—I don't think."

"If we make it that far," Q challenged Doc. "You've never operated one of those beasts and I'll lay odds this tub has 50 mm guns under those three tarps on her bow."

"But the hover craft can easily out-maneuver her," Doc countered.

"Yeah! When the operator knows how to operate her!" Q countered back.

"Don't overthink this, Q," Doc advised his friend. "What's the worst that could happen?"

"We could start World War III!" Q suggested.

"Besides that…" Doc said with an embarrassed laugh.

18

BREACHING THE DOOMSDAY VAULT

"This is serious." Louis jumped into the conversation. "You'll have to leave Lieutenant Ivanov on the island to avoid kidnapping him, and that's just one of the potential charges Russia could file with the world court. Are you sure you know what you're doing, Doc?"

"Honestly...no," Doc admitted. "But odds are Russia would never open that can of worms. No pun intended. How would they account for having built a Doomsday Vault in international waters? How would they explain ferrying us out there? I don't see that happening. So I'd say we have a plan to quickly and effectively evacuate the Keeper and every single Guardian he has with him back to the U.S. Will let President Preston handle the blow-back and ensure that Russia gets its landing craft back too, in exchange for allowing the U.S. to bring charges against the Keeper. He loves making deals like that."

"I hope you're right," Louis said, and dropped the matter.

"Let's run through what we know and expect about getting into the vault in the first place," Noah said.

"Based upon things we've seen Guardians do just outside the doors in satellite photos, it doesn't appear the vault is equipped with exterior surveillance cameras," Doc said.

"That's a huge plus for the element of surprise," Louis noted.

"So we'll park ourselves outside the doors and wait for them to open," Doc said. "When they do, we'll pounce, incapacitate whoever comes out with our PHASRs, bind and gag 'em, and slip inside before the doors automatically close behind us. As we start down the long entrance chamber toward the inner doors, the first person to see the door control panel will give a signal and will also be the one to open the doors for our exit."

"Roger that!" everyone replied.

"Make sure the safeties are off on your side arms and XRails," Doc reminded them, "but do not use either of them unless I do. If I do, open up and let 'em have it. I'll only allow it if we're in a desperate, life or death circumstance. Until then it's *PHASRs only*. Understood?"

"Understood," his teammates all replied.

"Assuming this strategy works as well as it did the last time, we should be able to get the drop on the Keeper and the Guardian with him. Twenty minutes should be more than enough time to gag and cuff them all. We each have a small backpack with a dozen handcuffs. When the targets regain consciousness, we'll march them to the front doors. Just before opening the back to the landing craft, we will incapacitate Lieutenant Ivanov with a

PHASR and cuff his wrists and ankles. With luck, we'll have the Keeper and his Guardians on U.S. soil by the time Commodore Tarkoff figures out what we've done. We'll leave the landing craft and Lieutenant Ivanov safe and sound on an Alaskan beach for the good Commodore to reclaim. No harm, no foul! Then we'll hand the Keeper and his Guardians over to the U.S. Air Force! Mission accomplished!"

"Sounds simple enough," Louis said almost convincingly. Even as he spoke, he recalled reading that Prussian Field Marshal Helmuth Karl Bernhard Graf von Moltke went down in military history for having said, "No battle plan ever survives contact with the enemy."

"Let's grab our gear and get this operation underway."

Lieutenant Ivanov soon saw the team reemerge on the main deck with their gear.

"Are you preparing to leave?" he shouted to them.

"Ready when you are!" Doc shouted back.

The lieutenant scrambled aboard the landing craft and bounded into the operator's chair.

"Strap in for the ride of your lives!" he shouted over his shoulder to Doc and his teammates, as they stowed their weapons in a chest at the very back of the cabin and took seats in the rear of the large cabin that sat well above and off to one side of the open-air main cargo area.

The four huge turbine engines roared to life with increasing volume and power and the craft rose to about six inches above the surface of the water. The four Americans all thought at once of how much the floating sensation of the craft mimicked the Chinook choppers they'd ridden in so much recently.

"It feels like a helicopter!" Doc yelled to the young, stoic lieutenant.

"In many ways the dynamics are the same!" the young Russian shouted back. "After months of training in a simulator, operators often say they feel qualified as helicopter pilots."

"I'm telling you, Doc, operating this thing by the seat of your pants is not a good idea," Q pressed harder this time, fearing a wrong move while trying to escape could jeopardize the mission.

"It may not be a good idea," Doc replied, "but it's the best one I have at the moment. Have some faith and go with it, Q. If this works, you might even get your picture taken with President Preston in the Oval Office."

"Big deal," Q grunted. "I didn't even vote for him."

"I didn't hear that," Doc said with a pained smile and a headshake.

"Geronimo!" Lieutenant Ivanov shouted as the craft spun 180 degrees and slid across the surface of the sea like a hockey puck on ice.

"No one says 'Geronimo' anymore," Q said to Doc with an eye-roll.

"Knock it off, Q," Doc told him. "Like it or not, he's our ticket to successfully completing this mission."

"I can't wait to see his face when he's in handcuffs," Q persisted.

The craft transitioned from sea to sand with almost no noticeable effect on its speed and maneuverability. The lieutenant cut the turbines and set the craft down on the beach about a mile east of the vault's huge steel double doors. Doc, Q, Noah, and Louis double-timed it up the beach and stretched out behind a dune that over-looked the bunker's entrance.

"Don't relax and let your guard down, men," Doc prompted them. "Those doors could open at any minute and we have no idea how many Guardians will exit when it does."

"Piece of cake," Q mumbled as he looked the entrance over carefully.

"Seems easy enough alright," Noah agreed.

"Give 'em hell first chance we get," Q grunted to them with a toothpick in his mouth.

"Now that's a master plan if ever I've heard one," Doc said sarcastically.

"*Someone* had to come up with one," Q grunted some more. "You can thank me later."

The team actually felt the ground rumble slightly before they heard the low growl of the heavy double doors opening.

"Ready or not," Doc whispered. "Wait for my command."

No reply was necessary or uttered as two Guardians, then three, then five, emerged from the bunker, set their weapons down, got comfortable, and lit cigarettes.

"Steady," Doc whispered.

Three more joined the first five and they all sat in a circle and gabbed and smoked.

"NOW!" Doc shouted, and sprinted over the dune with his three companions. "Shout as loud as you can, men!" he told them while running.

"Ahhhhhhh!" they all howled through their blacked-out visors to grab the unsuspecting Guardians by complete surprise and ensure they were looking directly at their attackers with eyes opened wide.

"Let's let 'em have it, Q!" Doc shouted as he and Q stopped dead and fired their PHASRs at the smokers' circle.

All eight Guardians fell like rag dolls, sound asleep like newborn babes.

"Cuff 'em quick and move on into the vault." Doc shouted. "The faster we do this the more certain our success will be! Move in silence from here on out!"

The four of them silently slipped through the doors and Louis located the control panel. As the doors rumbled closed, Doc turned to Louis and signaled him to open the double inner doors that stood between the team and their targets. The inner doors moved more smoothly and almost silently. So Doc and company were able to advance quite a few steps before one of the Guardians spotted them and shouted to the others.

"Kill them!" he screamed at the top of his lungs before he and his companions were blasted to sleep by the PHASRs. The first wave was conquered and cuffed in moments.

Doc then signaled the team to fire their PHASRs upward into the girders that supported the vault's rock ceiling and lighting system. Another half dozen Guardians fell unconscious to the floor of the vault. There was a high degree of risk of injury or even death, but Doc didn't have time to devise a better plan. They too were quickly cuffed and Doc and company moved to the very rear of the large one-room bunker where they found offices stretching from one side of the concrete cavern to the other. Each team member kicked in the door of one office or another and bathed the interiors with the PHASR rays, then cuffed however many Guardians fell unconscious under fire.

It was Doc who found the Keeper, cowering beneath a desk in the last office checked.

"You're lucky I don't kill you, you dirty, rotten son of a bitch!" Doc shouted as he blasted the Keeper with his PHASR and the maniac collapsed in a heap. Doc moved in and cuffed the Keeper and hefted him over his shoulder in a fireman's carry.

"We've got him, gentlemen!" he shouted to his team members triumphantly.

The team stood vigil over the Keeper and twenty-two of his Guardians who slowly awoke and regained their senses. When they could all stand, the team headed them out of the vault. Outside, Louis uncuffed the eight smokers' ankles and they fell in with the crowd as they marched toward the landing craft.

"You will pay with your lives for this!" the Keeper spat at Doc and his comrades.

"Shut up, Baird!" Doc barked back at Baird. "Save your breath for the judge who sends you to the electric chair, which is too lenient a punishment if you ask me!"

"You will never lock me up, Doc!" Baird shouted. "You can't match wits with me!"

"Oh, no?!" Doc replied more quietly. "Which of us is wearing handcuffs?"

"You will never take me in!" Baird continued to yell.

"Just keep walking, you maniac," Doc answered.

At the landing craft, Lieutenant Ivanov helped load

the Guardians and Baird into the cargo area and Doc and Q zapped them all with the PHASRs once again so they would sleep during what was surely going to be a wild ride to the mainland.

"Let's get going!" Doc yelled to the lieutenant, who then shoved the throttle forward and spun the hulking craft around toward the sea.

Once they were over open water. Doc walked up behind the lieutenant, spun him around by the shoulder, and blasted him at point blank range with the PHASR.

With the last of the PHASR blasting over, Doc and the rest of the team took off their helmets. Doc pushed the lieutenant's limp body out of the operator's chair and took his place at the controls.

"Hang on, gentlemen!" Doc shouted over his shoulder. "ETA for Wales, Alaska, is eighteen minutes! Call for the chopper to meet us on the beach outside Wales! Geronimo!"

Q knew Doc shouted "Geronimo!" for his benefit and it made him laugh to see his friend act like a boy with a new toy train on Christmas morning. Doc's escape plan worked flawlessly for the next five minutes. Then suddenly, *50 Years of Victory* was on their tail and firing hot 50 mm shells at them from the big guns on its bow. Moving at more than 40 knots, the noise from the landing craft's four big turbines faded behind it. So Doc could hear the 50 mm shells whistling through the air well over the craft as a command to stop or be sunk. Doc bet that the Commodore would not sink the $28 million landing craft as long as he thought there was a chance he would catch up to it.

But the shots got more threatening—and potentially deadly—when Doc did not slow the craft to allow the Commodore to overtake it. Doc heard several shells whiz so close he thought he'd be hit at any moment. So he began wild, elusive maneuvers, zigzagging left and right and looping back to actually sweep the craft in a huge circle around the ice breaker. The deadly game of cat and mouse went on for more than twenty minutes and Doc knew he needed at least another ten minutes to reach the Alaskan shore...if he would ever reach it at all.

Then suddenly, as if it was sent by God himself, a fast and deadly *U.S. Navy Mark VI* patrol boat appeared out of nowhere, racing through the water at more than 40 knots. It very deliberately cut a wickedly close path just ten yards or less away from the ice breaker's bow. When three such harrowing passes did not divert or slow the Russian vessel, the *Mark VI's* crew fired rockets across its bow until the Commodore finally took them serious, slowed the ice breaker to a crawl, and watched from a distance where the landing craft put in on the shore. The *Mark VI* then trailed the landing craft about 200 yards behind and the two vessels headed to the Alaskan coast. Meanwhile, the captives were coming to their senses and beginning to try to stand in the rocking and swaying hover craft.

"Put your helmets back on and zap 'em one more time!" Doc shouted to his team.

Doc caught sight of the Keeper struggling to his feet in the craft's rearview mirror. Q, Noah, and Louis seemed not to have heard Doc's call for them to zap the prisoners again. While Doc fought to keep the craft headed to the coast, he watched the maniac in the mirror and saw him stumble to the inflated five-foot-high cargo area's rear sidewall.

"Somebody zap him quick!" Doc screamed over his shoulder.

But it was too late. The Keeper awkwardly leapt and tumbled over the sidewall into the churning surf behind the hover craft. Doc quickly pulled back on the throttle. But a *Mark VI* crewmember waved him on, signaling that they would fish the Keeper out of the water and—Doc assumed—bring him ashore shortly.

After Doc shut off the craft's huge turbines and it came to rest on the beach, he anxiously surveyed the waters off the shore but there was no trace of the *Mark VI*. As Noah, Q, and Louis managed the process of moving the Guardians from the craft to the beach, a large lump formed in Doc's throat and he panicked. The Keeper seemed to have vanished, and there was nothing Doc could do about it. His heart pounded and his mind raced. Was this possibly another one of the Keeper's illusions? Was the ship that intervened really a U.S. Navy patrol boat? Where did it come from? Were its crew really sailors? Could the Keeper be so crafty that he'd even thought of such an elaborate escape? Or did he drown because he hadn't anticipated being handcuffed?

"Keep your eyes on this bunch until the chopper arrives!" Doc yelled to his partners as he restarted the powerful turbines of the landing craft and stirred it back onto the water. "I've got to try to find the Keeper!"

As the chopper arrived, Doc cruised the coastline and scanned the waves in search of any sign that the Keeper was still in the water. He saw none. His perch, high in the enclosed cockpit of the hover craft, gave him a catbird seat view of a great expanse of water in the bright sunshine. Equally puzzling was how fast that Navy patrol boat had appeared and disappeared.

Doc couldn't fathom what had just happened or even begin to understand how it had happened. He felt as though he'd dropped what would have been the winning touchdown pass with no time left on the clock in the only Super Bowl performance of his life. Time had indeed run out. Q, Louis, and Noah had loaded all the Guardians onto the chopper and it was perched to take off as soon as he returned to the beach and climbed aboard.

But Doc scoured the waves for another half hour and hoped beyond hope that somehow, someway, he would either find the Keeper or some evidence that he was at the bottom of the Bering Strait, and not laughing at him in some ingenious hiding place. Doc was painfully aware that Wales had the only airstrip within hundreds of miles. As short as the strip was, it was long enough to accommodate a small corporate jet that could quickly and easily transport the Keeper to any of the half dozen or more larger airports in the state, where he could board a larger jet and fly just about anywhere in the world. And Doc knew he wouldn't be able to live with himself if the Keeper pulled off such a diabolical illusion on his watch, right under his nose.

While Doc futilely crisscrossed the perimeter of the area where the Keeper went into the water, *50 Years of Victory* slowly advanced and was now roughly a half mile away and loomed like a hungry vulture waiting for its prey to die. Commodore Tarkoff was as determined to recover his lost landing craft as Doc was determined to recover his lost most wanted prisoner. That day, the Commodore ultimately headed home with that which he had lost. But Doc did not.

Out of time and options, Doc finally set the landing craft back down on the shore and ran to the chopper.

"Go without me!" he yelled to the pilot. "Pick me up tomorrow at the same time unless you hear otherwise from the President!"

"What the hell are you doing, Doc?" Q shouted from the chopper's open side door. "Have you lost your mind? The Keeper's probably drowned. Or else he's miles away! Either way, you're going home without him...whether today or tomorrow. So get in now and let us get out of here, damn it!"

But Doc stubbornly signaled the pilot to take off without him, and then watched it ascend and fade into the bright sunlit sky. When he could no longer see or hear the big chopper, he made his way to the high ground he could find overlooking the village's half-mile-long air strip, and hunkered down in the tall grass for the vigil he vowed he'd mount for the next twenty-four hours. He stalwartly held that high ground like a watchman on a wall, expending his last ounce of strength and commitment, defending a world that wanted only to get through each day without fear of the suffering and pain evil men can inflict for whatever reason...or no reason at all.

Doc made himself as comfortable as possible on the hard ground. He had rations and water for the long hours ahead. He studied and restudied his PHASR, XRail, and Wilson Combat 1911 pistol to occupy his mind and pass the time. When night came, Doc fought off the draining seduction to sleep even for half an hour, fearing he might miss the approach of a small, single-engine plane under the cover of darkness...as dangerous as that maneuver would be in the mountains of Alaska's coast. But a plane never came. Did the Keeper know he was watching?

As Doc asked himself that question, he began to question his own sanity. Had he sat on the cold, hard ground, and laid in the tall grass through a long, frigid, sleepless night, out of a commitment to see justice done...or an obsessive need to believe the evil monster who had consumed his every thought for months must still be alive and could be caught, which would prove those months hadn't been foolishly wasted?

By sunrise, Doc's sanity had been restored. He reasoned that shortly after yesterday's raid on the vault, the government must have learned enough—or presumed enough—to decide there was no reason to extract Doc earlier than he'd told the chopper pilot to return. They must have concluded that the Keeper had either drowned or escaped. Either scenario meant Doc had needlessly wasted a lot of time and missed a lot of sleep, with no hope of catching the madman.

So Doc was more than ready to climb aboard when the chopper finally returned. But he still raged inside as the chopper lifted him off the beach. He continued to struggle with the unforgiving reality that the circumstances surrounding the Keeper's disappearance were not only completely beyond his control, but weren't even fully understandable. Worst of all, the circumstances had defeated him.

The noble warrior braced himself and stood at the chopper's open side door as the mighty fighting machine lifted him 200 feet above the coastline and cruised out over the Bering Strait one last time. Doc surveyed the sea below a final time, certain that it was either the Keeper's final resting place...or the battlefield where he'd suffered the worst, most humiliating defeat of his entire life. Whatever the case, Doc had done the best he could and was finally going home.

19

ONE GOOD REASON

Reunited once again as Doc stepped off the CH-47F onto Runway Four at Eielson Air Force Base, just south of Fairbanks, Louis, Noah, and Q were as thrilled as Doc to finally be headed home. They missed their wives and all the other things that made their chaotic, unpredictable lives worth living.

"This is probably going to sound weird, but I'm awfully glad to see you guys," Doc said as he raised his arms to pull them into a loose huddle as brothers.

"We're mighty glad to see you too, Doc," Louis said with his trademark flawless smile.

"Same goes for me, Doc," Noah said with a smile and a headshake. "But I don't understand why you always have to make these grand, dramatic entrances instead of arriving at the same time as the rest of us."

"Well, somebody had to stay behind and mop up the mess you made," Doc said jokingly.

"We kinda figured you maybe stayed behind because

you'd gotten attached to the area," Noah teased Doc just a little more.

"Not at all," Doc assured him. "Believe me when I say Dorothy was right. there's no place like home!"

Then, as was becoming a tradition of its own, Q handed Doc the sword cane he'd given to him as a gift months before and simply uttered the words, "Let's go home, Doc."

"I'm all for that," Doc sighed. "But first I need a hot shower and a change of clothes."

"We gotcha covered on that front," Louis chuckled as the team led dock to Hanger #3 where President Preston's personal 757 was fueled and ready to take off when they were.

"Your gear's already aboard, Doc," Noah said. "We stowed your duffle in the forward bedroom, thinking you'd want to use the walk-in shower with the half dozen shower heads."

"Supper will be served as soon as you shower and dress," Q told Doc. "You've got your choice of a twenty-ounce porterhouse steak with all the sides, or classic Cajun jambalaya, or President Preston's personal favorite: mac and cheese."

Three flight attendants cheerfully greeted the men as they stepped onto the plane.

"Good afternoon, gentlemen!" the attendant named Rosalee said. "Can I get you a beverage and perhaps a light snack or appetizer before we serve dinner?"

"I'd love a cold beer," Doc said as he headed in the direction of the front bedroom.

"Certainly, sir," Rosalee replied. "I'll set it just outside the bedroom door so that you may enjoy it before, during, or after you shower. Have you made your choice for supper?"

"I'll have the porterhouse, well done, with broccoli and baked sweet potato," Doc told her. "Thank you so much. And please call me Doc."

"You got it, Doc!" the attendant happily answered. "And you can call *me* Rosy!"

A half hour later, Doc rejoined the team in the main cabin and stretched out in a luxurious recliner. His three partners were watching videotape highlights of the New England Patriots' latest Super Bowl victory.

"Hey fellas," Doc said, "can you please pause that for a few minutes? Rosy just informed me that the President wants a brief videoconference with us. And his staff has arranged a videoconference with the wives too, before we eat."

"Now we're talking!" Louis said, and handed the remote to Rosy and she set up the call.

"Hello again, fellas!" the President boomed on the 84-inch flat screen on the forward wall of the main cabin. "Does the smile on my face look genuine?" the President asked them. "It should, because your excellent efforts have made me a happier man, made the U.S. a safer country...and frankly, have made the entire world a safer place! I'd say that's three for three!"

"Thank you, Mr. President," Doc said humbly. "But we left Alaska without Jonah Baird. So please elaborate on why the world's a safer place."

"We've got him, Doc!" the President gushed with an impish, satisfied grin.

"You've got whom?" Doc asked with a touch of aggravation.

"Jonah Baird! The Keeper!" the President boomed with his arms open wide.

"How?" was all Doc could say as he scanned the faces of his partners, hoping they had a clue regarding what the President was congratulating them for.

"That Navy patrol boat fished him out of the water, but he jumped back into the drink about ten miles out from where he gave your team the slip," the President explained. "The Navy lost him too and he swam ashore, spent the night in a field, and nearly froze to death. The experience shook him up so bad he hiked to the nearest sheriff's office this morning and turned himself in for a hot shower and dry clothes. He didn't even use an alias. And he gave up the secret word that tells the Guardians to stand down. Law enforcement worldwide is rounding them up as we speak. You guys hit a game-winning grand slam. You're all incredible!

"I've got no other work for you fellas. So take some well-earned time off. Whether you do that separately or as a group, my plane will be available if you need it. Just say the word. Of course, there will be a little something extra in your pay envelopes to help with the vacation. And Master Sergeant Danforth, I've also signed and sent letters of promotion for you and your wife, Sergeant Danforth, to your COs. But the two of you will continue to report to Doc for the foreseeable future...at least, as long as I'm your Commander in Chief."

"Thank you! Thank you very much, Mr. President!"

Louis said breathlessly. "Jenny will be very pleased to hear the news."

"She already knows," the President said. "I took the liberty of having a similar video conference with your wives just minutes ago. Please do me the favor of talking with them about having lunch and taking photos with Melanie and me here at the White House soon and send my staff a few dates that you all can be here. They'll confirm a date with you and make all the arrangements. We will be pleased and honored to meet everyone and show our appreciation for all you've done for the nation. That's all I have for now, gentlemen. Unless you have questions, I've got other work to attend to."

"No questions, Mr. President!" the men said in unison.

"God bless you, fellas! Have a great day!" he said, and ended the call.

"Wow!" was all Louis could say, and his eyes were wide with wonder.

"Looks like you and Noah are going to the White House with us," Q said cheerfully.

"It'll be a trip to remember. I can tell you that," Doc said. "Well, it's time to call the wives and share the excitement."

All four men smiled like Cheshire cats as Rosie made the connection and their wives appeared on the screen seated in the kitchen of Doc and Connie's place on Flathead Lake.

"We're almost home, Beauty!" Doc called out with his arms straight up in the air.

"I know, John! I'm so happy to see you and the fellas!"

Connie replied. "Have you spoken with the President? He told us he thinks you all are the greatest thing that's happened to the country since he got elected!"

"That sounds like him, alright!" Q said, and laughed. "I miss you, Marsha! Please have some big hugs and kisses ready for me when I finally get back!"

"I will, Q, darling," Marsha gushed. "The President didn't tell us what you did. But he sure is glad you did it. I'm so proud of you and can't wait to see you."

"Hello, Madeleine darling!" Noah called out to his wife emotionally.

"Hello, Noah! It's wonderful to see your face!" she said, bouncing in her seat. "I'm so thankful you're safe and coming home! Get here fast so we can begin celebrating together!"

"I will sweetheart!" Noah said. "We're headed to Spokane now. See you soon, honey!"

"Hi, baby!" Louis shouted like the new groom he was. "I miss you so much and I can't wait to see you, Staff Sergeant Jenny Danforth!"

"Hello, Sergeant Major Danforth!" Jenny happily replied, and saluted her new husband. "I don't have the foggiest idea what you did, but it was enough to get us both promoted! I'm so excited that you'll be home tonight, Louis. Don't you dare stop for anything when you land in Spokane. Get here the moment you can. I love you! I miss you! And I'm proud of you!"

"We have very much to be thankful for, especially our future together," Louis said. "See you real soon, baby!"

Rosy signed off and ended the connection in order to begin serving supper and taking the team's drink orders.

As wonderful and extravagant as the setting was aboard the President's personal luxury 757, Doc still thought of it as merely a pleasant means of passing the time during the four-hour flight back to Spokane. He smiled at the thought of how austere the two-hour hitch aboard a puddle-jumper to his dock on Flathead Lake would seem after enjoying a hot shower, a well-done porterhouse, ice-cold beer, and conference calls aboard the President's personal 757. But the excitement to be returning to home overshadowed all else for Doc and the other members of the team. It was definitely time to shut out the world and reconnect with the people and things that really matter.

At the big lake house in Montana, Connie, Marsha, and Madeleine were walking on air. Jenny was too, but she was burdened and Connie saw it immediately and took her out to the front porch where they could talk quietly for a moment.

"What's wrong, dear?" she asked her newest close friend.

"I'm just struggling with selfish thoughts," Jenny answered.

"Too personal to share?" Connie asked.

"Not really. I'm thrilled for Louis. I truly am. But all of a sudden I feel like I'm just riding on his coattails," Jenny said. "He was out there putting it all on the line, while I stayed here safe and warm with you and Marsha and Madeleine. But we both got promoted. It doesn't seem fair to me, that's all. It's sure not what I signed up for as a wife and a Marine."

"Well, I don't know what to say about that," Connie

told her. "But I do agree with what Doc so often says—that everything happens for a reason."

"I try to believe that too," Jenny sighed. "And I feel crummy for pouting about getting promoted while I stayed back with you and Marsha and Madeleine. But I just can't imagine what possible reason there can be for it to have happened this way."

"Say, why don't you take a ride to the market with me?" Connie asked cheerfully. "The ride and fresh air and the scenery always cheer *me* up. Maybe it'll work for you too."

"I'd like that," Jenny said

After freshening up, the two of them hopped in Connie's Escalade and pulled beside Sergeant Peters and Corporal Woodson, the Homeland Security agents standing watch over the house that afternoon, to tell them when they expected to be back.

"Ride along with them," Peters said to Woodson. "It's bound to be more enjoyable than being stuck in this SUV with me."

The corporal jumped into the Escalade's back seat and the three of them headed to town.

"You sure have a beautiful place, Mrs. Holiday," the corporal said.

"Thank you," Connie replied. "And please call me Connie. This is Jenny Danforth and neither of us know your first name, Corporal."

"It's Franklin, ma'am...I mean Connie," he replied. "Sergeant Peters just learned that you'll be free of us soon...probably by the time your husbands return this evening. I guess you'll be glad when that happens. It's got to be creepy to have agents sitting outside your house day and night."

"A little," Connie agreed. "But believe me, we're grateful for the peace of mind it's given us, especially while we had no idea how events were unfolding. So it's been a mixed blessing, but a blessing nonetheless."

"Where are we headed?" Franklin finally thought to ask.

"To the market for some wine first and then a quick stop at the bank," Connie told him.

"Can you possibly stretch that out to last about four hours?" Franklin chuckled. "That would pretty much wind up my last shift with you wonderful ladies and it would be so much more enjoyable than climbing back into that Suburban with my grumpy partner."

"Well, we're not in any hurry," Connie said. "But I'm afraid it won't nearly take four hours to pick up some wine and stop by the bank."

"Well, I'm thankful for whatever break I get," Franklin chuckled again.

"What kind of wine do you like?" Jenny asked Franklin.

"I'm partial to a French merlot actually," Franklin said with a smile. "How about you?"

"That's my favorite too!" Jenny said with a broad smile.

"Well, we'll send you off with a nice bottle, then," Connie suggested. "What do you think your partner would like?"

"Why thank you so much, Connie," Franklin said

with genuine appreciation. "He'll get what I'm getting and be happy about it, I'm sure."

After making their wine selections at the market, they headed to the bank.

"I'm having supper catered at the house tonight and I need some cash to tip the servers," Connie explained as they entered the bank.

Franklin held the door for Jenny and Connie, then was suddenly pushed inside by a burly man and two others following close behind...with guns drawn.

"This is a hold-up!" one of the men shouted and fired his gun into the ceiling for effect. "Keep your hands where we can see them and do what you're told and no one will get hurt!"

"Everybody except teller number one get on the floor with your arms stretched out in front of you, NOW!" another of the men shouted.

Franklin lowered himself to the floor carefully so the 45 automatic in his shoulder holster didn't make a sound when it hit the floor. He caught the eyes of Connie and Jenny and signaled them to stay down just before he leapt to his feet, drew his 45, and shouted, "Homeland Security! Put down your weapons now!"

Connie's heart felt like it was going to pound its way out of her chest. She hoped some member of the bank's staff had pulled a silent alarm, and the police were about to arrive. Jenny had a different reaction. She was intently watching Franklin and the robbers' every move, looking for a way to help Franklin take and maintain control of the situation.

"Fuck you!" the robber standing over her shouted, and pointed his gun at Franklin.

When Jenny heard Franklin's 45 jam, her hand-to-hand combat training kicked in and she forcefully kicked the robber's nearest ankle, sending him crumbling to the floor. His 9mm pistol clanged to the floor and slid close enough for Jenny to grab it. In a heartbeat, she was on her feet, took aim, and shot the pistol another robber was holding right out of his hand.

"The next one will hit flesh and bone!" she said convincingly. "Anyone want to test me?"

No one made a sound as Jenny strode to the third robber, yanked his pistol free from his hand, and tucked it into her belt. The police suddenly burst in the door with guns drawn.

"Police! Nobody move!" one of them yelled.

Jenny raised her hands along with Franklin and the robbers she'd just disarmed.

"I'm Homeland Security Agent Franklin Woodson," Franklin said loudly. "My badge and ID are in my jacket's inside pocket. The ladies are with me."

"Everyone sit on the floor with your hands behind your head until we sort this out!" a police officer said.

It did get sorted out and Connie and company returned to the lake house. Franklin and Corporal Woodson were assigned to other duty about an hour later, bid the ladies goodbye, and left with their imported merlot tucked safely in the rear of their Suburban.

The seaplane carrying Doc, Q, Louis, and Noah pulled up to the dock just in time for supper and the men brought more than enough joy to the lake house to make up for the time they had been away. While they sampled the wine selected by Jenny and Connie that afternoon and waited for the caterer to arrive with supper, Connie told the story of how Jenny had foiled the bank robbery.

"The police sergeant told us there are arrest rewards out for two of the three knuckleheads Jenny got the drop on," Connie said. "So she and Louis will soon have more money for the down payment on that house they want to build."

"And how exactly did you get the drop on three guys with their guns drawn, starting from a prone position on the floor?" Q asked. "That's an amazing feat, even for a Marine."

"Oh really?" Jenny said, pretending to take offense.

"Yes, really," Q replied, and jokingly fanned the flame.

"You should be happy about it, instead of so cynical." Jenny turned serious.

"Well, give me one good reason," Q challenged her.

Determined to not let even the slightest well-intentioned poking and teasing spoil the special glow of their time together, Connie quickly rose to the occasion.

"We're all here together, safe and sound, cozy and warm, and closer than ever," Jenny said in a single breath.

Q paused and appeared to give it his most earnest thought of the evening.

"Is that all just one single reason?" Q said, trying to be both humorous and contrary.

"Sure sounds like one single good reason to me," Noah chimed in.

"Oorah!" Louis called out in agreement.

Seizing the moment, Doc quickly rose to his feet and raised his glass of wine.

"To one good reason!" he said as everyone rose with their glasses raised.

"To one good reason!" they all pronounced, and clinked their fine crystal wine glasses.

And at that moment, in the midst of that warm, joyous gathering of extraordinarily close and faithful friends and lovers, all was right in the world again.

EPILOGUE

A month later, the White House luncheon was the most memorable yet. Doc and Connie were accompanied by Louis and Jenny, Marsha and Q, and Noah and Madeleine. And Raymon and Thomas Byrnes were invited as well.

"If this keeps up, we'll need a bigger table," President Preston joked as he and Melanie entered their beautiful personal dining room.

After introductions, photos, and several minutes of small talk, the President asked them to have a seat and said, "Melanie and I could not be prouder or more pleased to have you all here. This is our opportunity to personally thank you for your sacrifice and service to the nation and the world. The commitment and courage displayed by each of you is truly extraordinary.

"Ladies, I promise you that my administration will never take your sacrifice, patience, and trust for granted. The role you play in your husbands' lives—and in their important efforts on behalf of our nation—is vital and indispensable. And men, though your heroic and selfless service to your country is only celebrated on a need-to-know basis, I can assure you that those who know are grateful beyond words

"And I wish to express special thanks to the Byrnes brothers for their tenacity in bringing the Keeper's plot to the attention of folks who perhaps should have recognized it sooner, but didn't. Connie, I've called you brave before, but since hearing about how you handled a hunting rifle under fire, I'm even more impressed. And Jenny, your quick action may very well have saved many lives on the very day the rest of us thought the danger had passed.

"What a group you are! Our nation is blessed to have you! Let's eat!"

It took two Suburbans to ferry the guests back to their hotels after lunch. As always Doc and Connie stayed at the Willard Inter-Continental Hotel three blocks from the White House. Marsha and Q, Noah and Madeleine, and Louis and Jenny stayed there as well. Thomas and Raymon had rooms at the Hotel Harrington, just three blocks farther up the street. So everyone was aboard when the Suburbans turned off 15th Street and Doc saw the Segway rental station on the corner. He reminded Connie it was on his "must do" list for their next visit.

"Look, Connie!" he said excitedly. "Let's do this."

"Oh, I don't know, John," Connie said, thinking no one was dressed for it.

"It'll be fun," he said, "and I always tell the guys I'm a man of my word."

Doc told the driver to pull over, asked his lunch

buddies to follow him, and rented Segways for everyone. After their incredible lunch, the unexpected joy rides were a hit. An hour was plenty of time to loop through Lafayette Square Park and take dozens of group pictures.

"You were right again, John," Connie admitted with her fabulous smile. "This is great!"

About a block from the Segway station, with ten minutes left on the rental, Doc's battery was running down. So he was well behind the pack when his cell phone rang.

"It's Doc," he simply said.

"Doc, you're probably going to hate me for this, but I must ask you to consider taking a trip to Arizona. Some guy near Sedona claims he's Nostradamus, believe it or not. It would be no big deal, but Jonah Baird claims the guy's his partner and they're going to finish what he started."

"But Baird's locked up," Doc said matter-of-factly.

"Not anymore," the President answered. "He escaped about an hour ago."

"I'll call you back shortly, Mr. President," Doc said. "Wish me luck breaking this to Connie...and go ahead and make the arrangements."

"Thanks, Doc," the President said. "I'm sorry you didn't get more of a break. But as you always say, everything happens for a reason."

Made in the USA
Columbia, SC
19 June 2020

11505685R00150